孤星血淚

Great Expectations

原著 _ Charles Dickens
改寫 _ Jennifer Gascoigne
譯者 _ 林育珊

U0025462

ABOUT THIS BOOK

For the Student

🎧 Listen to the story and do some activities on your Audio CD.

💬 Talk about the story.

⭐ Prepare for Cambridge English: Preliminary (PET) for schools.

For the Teacher

 A state-of-the-art interactive learning environment with 1000s of free online self-correcting activities for your chosen readers.

Go to our Readers Resource site for information on using readers and downloadable Resource Sheets, photocopiable Worksheets, and Tapescripts. www.helblingreaders.com

For lots of great ideas on using Graded Readers consult Reading Matters, the Teacher's Guide to using Helbling Readers.

Level 4 Structures

Sequencing of future tenses	*Could* / *was able to* / *managed to*
Present perfect plus *yet*, *already*, *just*	*Had to* / *didn't have to*
First conditional	*Shall* / *could* for offers
Present and past passive	*May* / *can* / *could* for permission *Might* for future possibility
How long?	*Make* and *let*
Very / *really* / *quite*	Causative *have* *Want* / *ask* / *tell someone to do something*

Structures from lower levels are also included.

CONTENTS

Charles Dickens was born in Portsmouth on 7th February, 1812. He was the second of eight children. His father, John Dickens, was a clerk[1] in the Navy[2]. In 1814 the Dickens family moved to London and two years later to Chatham in Kent. Charles attended a private[3] school for a few years there until the family moved back to London in 1822.

Two years later Charles's father was sent to a debtors'[4] prison for not paying his bills[5]. Charles was 12 years old at the time. The family had no money, so he had to leave school and get a job in a factory[6] that made shoe polish[7]. The conditions[8] there were very bad and the workers were very poor. It was a

completely different world from the one Charles knew and he was often sad and lonely.

His father managed to[9] leave the prison and Charles returned to school, but this experience had a great effect[10] on him. He never forgot it and described it in several of his novels.

When he was 15, he left school and started work as a clerk in a law office. Then he worked as a reporter in the law courts. In 1836 his first novel, *The Pickwick Papers*, was published. It was a great success and the beginning of his career as a novelist.

Charles Dickens is much loved for his great contribution[11] to classic English literature[12]. Some of his more well-known novels include *Oliver Twist* (1837), *A Christmas Carol* (1843), *David Copperfield* (1850) and *Great Expectations* (1860).

He died in 1870 and is buried at Westminster Abbey, London.

---

1 clerk [klɝk] (n.) 辦事員
2 navy [ˋnevɪ] (n.) 海軍
3 private [ˋpraɪvɪt] (a.) 私立的
4 debtor [ˋdɛtɚ] (n.) 債務人
5 bill [bɪl] (n.) 帳單
6 factory [ˋfæktərɪ] (n.) 工廠
7 polish [ˋpolɪʃ] (n.) 擦亮劑
8 conditions [kənˋdɪʃənz] (n.)〔複〕條件
9 manage to 設法
10 effect [ɪˋfɛkt] (n.) 影響
11 contribution [͵kɑntrəˋbjuʃən] (n.) 貢獻
12 literature [ˋlɪtərətʃɚ] (n.) 文學

Great Expectations is usually described as a *bildungsroman*, a type of novel that was popular in Victorian times[1]. *Bildungsroman* is a German[2] word used for novels that show the psychological[3] and moral[4] development of the main character as he or she grows up. However, *Great Expectations*, like most of Charles Dickens's novels, cannot be so easily defined[5]. It is also a story about love and passion[6], a mystery[7] story, and a story that comments on the society of the time.

Great Expectations is set[8] on the marshes[9] of Kent and in London in the early to mid-1800s. The main character is a poor orphan[10] boy called Pip, who lives with his older sister and her husband, Joe. One day he meets and falls in love with

a rich girl called Estella. She laughs at him because he is a poor village boy and he starts to become unhappy with his life.

A few years later he learns that he has a secret benefactor[11], who wants him to live the life of a gentleman. Now that he is rich, he thinks that he has a chance of winning Estella's love. He leaves his village and goes to live in London, where he makes new friends. He starts to feel ashamed[12] of his home and his family, particularly Joe, who he treats unkindly. However, after many adventures he is finally able to recognize his mistakes.

Charles Dickens originally wrote a sad ending for *Great Expectations* but he decided to change it to a happier one because of a suggestion from one of his friends. Most books today contain the new ending but there are some that also include the original one.

---

1 Victorian times 英國維多利亞時代（1837–1901 年）
2 German [ˈdʒɝmən] (a.) 德語的
3 psychological [ˌsaɪkəˈlɑdʒɪkl] (a.) 心理的
4 moral [ˈmɔrəl] (a.) 道德上的
5 define [dɪˈfaɪn] (v.) 定義
6 passion [ˈpæʃən] (n.) 戀情
7 mystery [ˈmɪstərɪ] (n.) 神祕事件
8 set [sɛt] (v.) 時空背景設定
　（三態：set; set; set）
9 marsh [mɑrʃ] (n.) 濕地
10 orphan [ˈɔrfən] (n.) 孤兒
11 benefactor [ˈbɛnəˌfæktɚ] (n.) 贊助人
12 ashamed [əˈʃemd] (a.) 羞愧的

1 Read the descriptions of some of the characters. Can you match them to the correct picture A to F? How do you know? Tell a friend.

_____ ① Herbert Pocket is a cheerful and kind boy and Pip's best friend.

_____ ② Estella Havisham is beautiful but cold and distant with Pip.

_____ ③ Abel Magwitch is a violent man but grateful to Pip for helping him.

_____ ④ Miss Havisham, a rich but unhappy woman, wants Pip to fall in love with Estella.

_____ ⑤ Joe Gargery is a simple, honest man and very kind to Pip.

_____ ⑥ Pip is a poor orphan who wants to change his life.

2 Read the sentences about the characters in Exercise **1**. Choose the correct definition of the colorful words.

_____ a Joe was the village blacksmith.
  1 someone whose job is to make things out of metal
  2 someone who works in a factory

_____ b Miss Havisham always wore her wedding dress and veil.
  1 thin piece of cloth worn over a woman's head
  2 thin scarf worn around a woman's neck

_____ c Estella was beautiful and also very proud.
  1 tall and very thin
  2 self-important, thinking yourself better than others

_____ d Abel Magwitch was an escaped convict when Pip first met him.
  1 someone who has run away from home
  2 someone who has been sent to prison

_____ e Herbert lived in a rather shabby building called Barnard's Inn.
  1 old and in bad condition
  2 with many floors

_____ f Pip dreamt of living the life of a gentleman.
  1 man of good social position
  2 man who is very kind

3 Look at the picture and find this character in other pictures in the book. Then answer the questions below.

Mr Jaggers

a What do you think his job is?

_____

b What do you think his relationship to Pip is?

_____

4 Read Pip's description of where he lived as a child. Tick (✓) the photo that best matches the description.

A

We lived in a village on the edge of the marshes. The land there was flat and without much vegetation because it was near the sea. It was a gray, windy, wild place.

5 Listen to Pip's description of his first impression of the city of London. Answer the questions.

a What was his general impression of the city?

_____

b What were the streets like?

_____

c What was the air like?

_____

d What covered everything?

_____

11

6 Pip grew up in the country and moved to London when he was a teenager. How do you think his life changed? Is it more fun to grow up in the country or in a big city? Discuss your ideas with a partner.

7 Read a modern definition of the word "expectations." Discuss the questions that follow it with a partner.

> **expectations** *[countable]* *[usually plural]*: a belief that something should happen in a particular way, or that someone or something should have particular qualities or behavior

(a) What expectations do you have of your friends?

Example   I expect my friends to help me when I have a problem.

b Think of an important person (or people) in your life who has (have) expectations for you—your parents, teachers, friends, football coach, boyfriend or girlfriend, etc. What are their expectations of you?

Example My parents expect me to study hard at school.

8 Discuss the following question with a partner.

a What do you think are the "expectations" in the title of the book?

_____

b Why do you think they are "great"?

_____

c Which character do you think has "great expectations"?

_____

1. A meeting in the churchyard

My father's family name was Pirrip, and my name is Philip. Because these names were difficult for me to say when I was a child, I called myself Pip. From then on I was known as Pip.

My parents were both dead and I lived with my sister. She was twenty years older than me and married to Joe Gargery, the local blacksmith[1]. He was a sweet-tempered[2], easy-going man with brown hair and blue eyes. My sister Mrs Joe Gargery was the opposite[3]. She had black hair and eyes and was very bad-tempered. She almost always wore an apron[4] over her dress because she was always busy. I often felt the power of her strong hands on the side of my head. Joe did too, but he never said anything to her. I couldn't understand why he married my sister—I suppose she made him.

We lived in a village on the edge[5] of the marshes. The land there was flat and without much vegetation because it was near the sea. It was a gray, windy, wild place.

---

1 blacksmith [ˋblæk͵smɪθ] (n.) 鐵匠
2 sweet-tempered [ˋswitˋtɛmɚd] (a.) 個性溫馴的
3 opposite [ˋɑpəzɪt] (n.) 相反面
4 apron [ˋeprən] (n.) 圍裙
5 edge [ɛdʒ] (n.) 邊緣

I found the grave[1] of my parents one foggy evening. It was half-hidden in the long grass of the old churchyard[2] about a mile from the village. I read the names on the tombstone[3]— Philip Pirrip and his wife Georgiana. Seeing them made me sad and I started to cry.

Suddenly a terrible voice shouted, "Be quiet! Or I'll cut your throat!"

I looked up and saw a man coming towards me out of the fog. He had no hat and old, broken shoes. His clothes were old and covered in mud[4] and there was a big iron ring[5] on his leg.

He took hold of my chin with one of his hands. I was very frightened.

"Oh! Don't cut my throat, sir," I cried. "Please don't, sir!"

"What's your name?" said the man. "Quick!"

"Pip, sir."

"What did you say?" said the man, putting his face close to mine. "Speak up!"

"Pip, sir."

"Where do you live?" he asked. "Show me!"

I pointed to the village in the distance.

1 grave [grev] (n.) 墓穴
2 churchyard [ˈtʃɜtʃˌjɑrd] (n.) 教堂墓地
3 tombstone [ˈtumˌston] (n.) 墓碑
4 mud [mʌd] (n.) 泥
5 iron ring 鐵環

The man looked at me for a moment. Then he picked me up, turned me upside down and emptied[6] my pockets. There was nothing in them, only a small piece of bread. After putting me on top of a tombstone, he took the bread and ate it hungrily. I was shaking with fear as I watched him. I had to try hard to stop myself from crying.

"Where's your mother?"

"Over there, sir!"

He started running away, but then stopped and looked over his shoulder.

"There, sir!" I explained, pointing to her grave. "Georgiana. That's my mother."

"Oh!" he said coming back. "And is your father there too?"

"Yes, sir," I replied.

"Who do you live with?" he asked.

"My sister, sir. Mrs Joe Gargery, wife of Joe Gargery, the blacksmith, sir."

"Blacksmith, eh?" he said and he looked down at the ring on his leg.

Then he took hold of my arms and pushed me backwards.

"Do you know what a file[7] is?"

"Yes, sir."

"And do you know what wittles[8] are?"

"Yes, sir."

---

6 empty [ˈɛmptɪ] (v.) 使空；倒空
7 file [faɪl] (n.) 銼刀
8 wittles [ˈwɪtl̩z] (n.)
〔舊〕〔俚〕〔複〕食物

"Well, get me a file and some wittles," he said, holding my arms tighter. "And bring them to me tomorrow morning early. And don't tell anyone that you have seen me. If you don't do exactly what I've told you, I'll cut out your heart, roast[1] it and eat it! Now, what do you say?"

He was hurting me, so I quickly agreed to do what he asked. Then he let me go. I sat and watched him as he limped[2] to the low churchyard wall and climbed over it. As soon as he disappeared in the darkness, I jumped off the tombstone and started to run. I didn't stop until I got home.

THE MAN

- Who do you think the man is?
- What is he doing in the churchyard?
- Why does he want a file?
- Is Pip going to tell anyone about him?

Joe's forge[3] was closed when I got back from the churchyard. I opened the kitchen door and went in. Joe was sitting there alone.

1 roast [rost] (v.) 烘烤
2 limp [lɪmp] (v.) 一瘸一拐地走
3 forge [fɔrdʒ] (n.) 鐵工廠；鐵鋪
4 stick [stɪk] (n.) 棍棒
5 burst in 突然進入（房間等）

"Mrs Joe is looking for you, Pip," he said. "She's been out several times."

"Has she?"

"Yes, Pip," said Joe. "And she's taken the stick[4] with her this time!"

Just at that moment the door opened and Mrs Joe burst in[5]. She looked very angry.

"Where have you been, you young monkey?" she shouted.
"Only to the churchyard," I replied.

"The churchyard!" she repeated. "What were you doing there at this time of night? I've spent the last hour looking for you! Worry and work! That's all I get for looking after you!"

She put the stick back in the corner and started to prepare tea. She cut two slices of bread, put some butter on them and gave one to Joe and the other to me. I remembered the terrible man in the churchyard and I was too afraid to eat mine. I knew that I had to keep it for him. So I quickly put it into the pocket of my trousers[1] while Joe wasn't looking.

The next day was Christmas Day. I got up before it was light and crept[3] downstairs. I stole some bread, some cheese and a beautiful pork pie[4]. The pie was a present from Uncle Pumblechook, a rich corn merchant[5] in the town. Then I went to the forge to get the file.

It was cold that morning and the fog was thicker than usual. When I got to the churchyard, I saw the man sitting on a tombstone in front of me. He seemed to be asleep, so I went up to him quietly and touched him on the shoulder. He jumped up immediately and I saw that it was a different man! He was dressed like the other one and he also had a big iron ring on his leg, but he was younger. When he saw me, he ran away quickly into the fog.

I walked a bit further into the churchyard and soon I saw the other one. Without saying anything, I handed him the file and the bag of food. He pushed the bread and the cheese into his mouth together, and then he started on the pie.

"I'm glad you like it," I said.

"I do, my boy. Thank you," he replied with his mouth full of pie.

"I have to go now," I said, but he wasn't listening.

He was too busy finishing the pie. I started to walk away. When I turned to look at him, he was trying to cut the ring off his leg with the file.

1 trousers ['traʊzəz] (n.) 〔複〕長褲
2 creep [krip] (v.) 躡手躡足地走
   （三態：creep; crept, creeped; crept, creeped）
3 pork pie 豬肉派
4 merchant ['mɜtʃənt] (n.) 商人

2. An arrest

Joe and I went to church later that morning while Mrs Joe got the Christmas dinner ready. There was a lot to do because she always invited Uncle Pumblechook and some neighbors to eat with us on Christmas Day.

At half past one we all sat down at the table. There were lots of delicious things to eat, but I was much too worried about the missing pork pie to enjoy them. Finally, the moment that I was dreading[1] arrived.

"Uncle Pumblechook has brought us a beautiful pork pie," Mrs Joe said with a big smile. "Would anyone like to try some?"

There was a chorus[2] of "Yes, please!," so she went to the kitchen to get it.

I couldn't stay there any longer. I had to escape[3]. I ran to the door, but I got no further. A police sergeant[4] and some soldiers were outside. They had guns and the sergeant was holding a pair of handcuffs[5].

---

1 dread [drɛd] (v.) 懼怕
2 chorus [korəs] (n.) 異口同聲
3 escape [əˋskep] (v.) 逃跑
4 sergeant [ˋsɑrdʒənt] (n.) 警官
5 handcuffs [ˋhænd͵kʌfs] (n.)〔複〕手銬

"Where's the blacksmith?" he asked.

Everyone inside stood up and followed Joe to the door. They were very curious.

"Can you repair these handcuffs, blacksmith?" the sergeant asked Joe. "The lock is broken. There are two convicts[1] on the marshes. They escaped from the prison ship last night. We must catch them before it gets dark. That's why we need the handcuffs."

Joe put on his leather apron and started work immediately. It didn't take him long to do the job.

"Here you are," he said, giving the handcuffs to the sergeant. "I'll come with you and help you look for the convicts. You can come too, Pip," he added.

We put on our coats and followed the sergeant and the soldiers to the churchyard. It was snowing now and very cold. Almost as soon as we got there, we heard voices in the distance[2]. Angry voices.

The soldiers immediately started running towards them with their guns ready. As we got nearer, the voices got louder. It was clear now that there were only two. I knew who they belonged to.

"Here they are!" shouted one of the soldiers. "Over here!"

---

1 convict [ˈkɑnvɪkt] (n.) 囚犯
2 distance [ˈdɪstəns] (n.) 遠處
3 ditch [dɪtʃ] (n.) 渠道
4 black and blue（打得）瘀青
5 villain [ˈvɪlən] (n.) 惡棍
6 torch [tɔrtʃ] (n.) 火把
7 hut [hʌt] (n.) 簡陋的小屋

The two men were in a muddy ditch[3]. They were fighting and didn't seem to notice us. The soldiers jumped in and pulled them apart. Then they put the handcuffs on them. Although the two men were covered in mud and blood, I recognized them immediately. The young man's face was black and blue[4]. He was very weak and a soldier had to help him stand up.

"He tried to murder me!" he said, looking at my convict.

"He's lying!" replied the other. "I caught him. I want him to go back to the prison ship. He's a villain[5]!"

The young man seemed to be afraid of his companion. He repeated weakly, "He tried to murder me!"

"Enough!" said the sergeant. "Light the torches[6]. We must take them back to the prison ship. Come on! Move!"

After walking for about an hour, we came to a wooden hut[7]. There was a guard in it and three or four soldiers. The sergeant wrote something in a book, and then the guard took the young man to the prison ship. While we were waiting in the hut, my convict stood in front of the fire thinking and looking at his feet. He never looked at me.

Suddenly he turned to the sergeant and said, "I want to say something. Can I speak?"

"You can say what you like," replied the sergeant.

"I took some wittles, from a house in the village over there. The one near the church. From the blacksmith's."

Joe looked at me in surprise.

"I was hungry so I took a pork pie and some bread," the convict said. Then he added, "I'm sorry. It was a very good pie."

"I'm glad you enjoyed it," said Joe kindly. "A man must eat."

Then the guard arrived to take him away. We stood at the window and watched as he climbed on the ship and disappeared.

PRISONS

- Where are, or were, these famous prisons? Choose from the countries in the list.

_____ a Alcatraz   1 France
_____ b Chateau d'If   2 French Guiana
_____ c Devil's Island   3 South Africa
_____ d Port Arthur   4 Tasmania
_____ e Robben Island   5 The USA

3. A visit to Satis House

One evening a year or two later, Mrs Joe returned from the market in town with some interesting news. Miss Havisham wanted me to go and play at her house! Joe and I looked at each other in surprise. Miss Havisham was a very rich woman who lived in a big house near the town. Although everyone knew her name, very few people knew what she looked like. She never went out.

"How does she know Pip?" asked Joe.

"Uncle Pumblechook told her about him," replied Mrs Joe. "He was at Satis House the other day. Miss Havisham told him that she was looking for a boy to come and play. He immediately suggested[1] Pip."

She started to fill a bowl with water.

"If the boy isn't grateful[2] tonight, he never will be! Come here, Pip!"

She took me by the shoulders and pushed my head into the water.

"Uncle Pumblechook's waiting outside for you in his carriage[3]," she said, as she scrubbed[4] my face.

---

1 suggest [sə`dʒɛst] (v.) 建議
2 grateful [`gretfəl] (a.) 感激的
3 carriage [`kærɪdʒ] (n.) 馬車
4 scrub [skrʌb] (v.) 用力擦洗

Soon I was clean from head to toe and dressed in my best clothes. After saying goodbye to Joe, I climbed in the carriage next to Uncle Pumblechook and we set off for the town.

At ten o'clock the next day I was outside the gates of Satis House. When I rang the bell, a young girl appeared. She was very pretty and suddenly I felt shy.

"Are you Pip?" she said.

From the way she spoke to me, I understood that she was not only beautiful but also very proud.

She let me in and I followed her silently across the courtyard[1] and into the house. We went along a lot of dark corridors[2] and then up some stairs. Finally we came to a door.

"Knock before you go in!" the girl said and went away.

I found myself in a large room lit[3] by many candles. All the clocks in the room read twenty to nine but it was already past ten.

Miss Havisham was sitting in an armchair near a small table. She was wearing a wedding dress made of rich materials[4] and a veil over her head. There were pale flowers in her white hair. But the bride[5] was no longer a young woman. Her dress and veil were no longer white, but yellow with age. The flowers in her hair were no longer fresh; their colors were no longer bright.

---

1 courtyard [ˈkortˌjɑrd] (n.) 庭院；天井
2 corridor [ˈkɔrɪdər] (n.) 走廊
3 light [laɪt] (v.) 照亮 (三態：light; lighted, lit; lighted, lit)
4 material [məˈtɪrɪəl] (n.) 質料
5 bride [braɪd] (n.) 新娘子

"Who is it?" she said.

"Pip, ma'am[1]."

"Come nearer! I want to look at you."

I stood in front of her and she looked at me. Then she put her hands on her left side.

"Do you know what I'm touching here?" she asked.

"Your heart, ma'am."

"Broken!" she said.

There was a long silence. Then she said, "Call Estella!"

I felt embarrassed calling the girl's name. She didn't reply immediately, but eventually she appeared.

"Come here, my dear," said Miss Havisham. "Play cards with this boy."

Estella looked shocked. "But he is a village boy! Look at his rough[2] hands!"

I thought I heard Miss Havisham whisper[3] to her, "Well? You can break his heart." But I wasn't sure.

We sat down and started to play. I made many mistakes because Estella made me feel stupid and clumsy[4]. Naturally, she won that game. She won the next game too. And the third. I was glad when Miss Havisham told me I could go home.

"Come again next week," she said. "Estella! Give him something to eat before he leaves."

---

1 ma'am [mæm] (n.) 夫人（= madam）
2 rough [rʌf] (a.) 粗糙的
3 whisper [ˈhwɪspɚ] (v.) 低聲說
4 clumsy [ˈklʌmzɪ] (a.) 笨拙的

Estella told me to wait for her in the courtyard. A few minutes later she returned with some bread and meat. She put them on the ground in front of me. I felt like a dog in disgrace[1] and I started to cry. She said nothing, but there was a triumphant[2] look on her face as she walked away.

I lay in bed that night and thought about my day at Satis House. It was a new world for me. Miss Havisham and Estella were not like the people in my village. They didn't have rough hands or eat in the kitchen. I began to feel ashamed of Joe, my sister and my home. I wanted to belong to the world of the people in Satis House.

1 disgrace [dɪsˋgres] (n.) 丟臉；蒙羞
2 triumphant [traɪˋʌmfənt] (a.) 勝利的
3 relative [ˋrɛlətɪv] (n.) 親戚
4 slap [slæp] (v.) 摑

4. A fight

The following Wednesday I returned to Satis House. That day there were some people in one of the rooms downstairs. From their conversation I guessed that they were Miss Havisham's relatives[3].

While Estella was taking me upstairs to Miss Havisham's room, she suddenly asked me, "Well! What do you think of me?"

"I think you are very pretty," I replied, "and a little unkind."

Then she suddenly slapped[4] my face. "What do you think of me now?" she said.

"I'm not going to tell you, miss."

She turned and walked away, leaving me outside Miss Havisham's door.

I went in. Miss Havisham was sitting next to the small table as usual.

"Ah, Pip," she said. "The days have passed quickly. Are you ready to play?"

"I don't think I am, ma'am," I replied.

"Well, if you don't want to play," she said, "you must work. Go and wait for me in the room opposite[1] this one."

Like all the other rooms in the house, that room was lit only by candles. I could see a long table with a white cloth[2] on it. There was a wedding cake in the middle of the table, but it was completely covered in large cobwebs[3].

Miss Havisham came in quietly and put her hand on my shoulder. We walked slowly around the table for a few minutes and then she said, "Did you see those people downstairs, Pip? They're my relatives, the Pockets. They come here once a year to visit me. They hope I will leave them my money when I die."

I didn't know what to say. Luckily Estella arrived at that moment and we went back to Miss Havisham's room to play cards.

I decided to have a look around the garden before going home that day. To my surprise I met a boy there. He was about the same age as me. He had a pale[4] face and fair[5] hair.

"Come and fight!" said the pale young gentleman when he saw me.

---

1 opposite [ˈɑpəzɪt] (prep.) 在對面
2 cloth [klɔθ] (n.) 布
3 cobweb [ˈkɑbˌwɛb] (n.) 蜘蛛網
4 pale [pel] (a.) 蒼白的
5 fair [fɛr] (a.) （頭髮）金色的

I didn't know what to do. I was afraid of hurting him because he didn't look very strong. However, he seemed determined[1] to fight, so I hit him. He fell to the ground and his nose started bleeding[2].

The next moment he was back on his feet ready to continue the fight. I hit him again, harder. I probably hit him three or four more times before he gave in.

"You've won," he said.

"Are you alright?" I asked. "Can I help you?"

"No, thank you," he replied. "Good afternoon!"

I continued to visit Satis House regularly[3] after that. Estella was always there. Sometimes she was almost kind to me, but most of the time she behaved coldly towards me. Her moods could change very quickly and I often didn't know what to say to her. Miss Havisham seemed to enjoy my confusion[4].

ESTELLA

- What is the relationship between Estella and Miss Havisham?

- Why is Estella so unfriendly to Pip?

- Why does Miss Havisham want Estella and Pip to be friends?

Mrs Joe and Uncle Pumblechook thought that Miss Havisham had plans for my future. They were always talking about what she might do for me. It made me angry, but secretly I hoped that they were right.

Then one day Miss Havisham said, "You are getting tall, Pip. It's time for you to start work."

She knew that Joe wanted me to work in the forge with him—to be his apprentice[5].

"Ask Mr Gargery to come here with the contract[6] for your apprenticeship. I'd like to see it."

"What time shall I tell him to come, ma'am?"

"I know nothing about times," she said. "Tell him to come soon. And you can come with him."

Joe and I returned together two days later. Joe looked very out of place[7] in Miss Havisham's room. I felt embarrassed and ashamed of him. When Miss Havisham asked him questions about his plans for me, he spoke to me instead of speaking to her! I saw a cruel smile on Estella's lips as she listened from behind Miss Havisham's chair. I wanted to run away.

Finally the documents[8] for my apprenticeship were signed and we were free to leave.

---

1 determined [dɪˋtɝmɪnd] (a.) 堅決的
2 bleed [blid] (v.) 流血
　（三態：bleed; bled; bled）
3 regularly [ˋrɛgjələlɪ] (adv.) 經常地
4 confusion [kənˋfjuʒən] (n.) 困惑
5 apprentice [əˋprɛntɪs] (n.) 學徒
6 contract [ˋkɑntrækt] (n.) 契約
7 out of place 不合適
8 document [ˋdɑkjəmənt] (n.) 文件

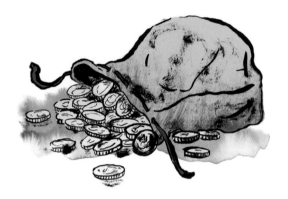

"Pip!" said Miss Havisham giving me a small bag. "Give this to your master. There are twenty-five guineas[1] in it. You have earned them. Goodbye, Pip."

Estella took us to the gate and let us out. Then she turned and went back inside without saying anything to me.

Mrs Joe was very happy when we showed her the guineas. On the day I became Joe's apprentice, she insisted[2] on having dinner in town at the Blue Boar Inn. She also invited Uncle Pumblechook. Everyone enjoyed the evening, but I didn't. Although Joe was the best and kindest man in the world, I had a strong feeling that his work was not the work for me.

---

1 guinea ['gɪnɪ] (n.) 基尼（英國舊時的一種硬幣）
2 insist [ɪn'sɪst] (v.) 堅持
3 do well 做得不錯
4 now and then 有時；偶爾

5. Great expectations

Joe and I usually went for a walk on the marshes on Sundays. It was pleasant and quiet there. As I watched the ships on the river, I often thought about my visits to Satis House. I couldn't forget Estella.

One Sunday I said to Joe, "I think I should go and see Miss Havisham. I'd like to thank her for helping me. Can I have a half-day holiday tomorrow, Joe?"

We weren't very busy, so he agreed.

I went the following afternoon. Miss Sarah Pocket opened the gate and took me upstairs to Miss Havisham's room. Everything there was the same as before.

"I hope you don't want anything," Miss Havisham said. "You'll get nothing."

"I only came to tell you that I'm doing well[3] at the forge," I replied. "I'm very grateful to you."

"Well, you can come and visit me now and then[4]—come on your birthday."

She saw me looking around the room.

"Estella isn't here," she said. "She's abroad[1]. She's learning to be a lady. She's prettier than ever, Pip. Do you miss her?"

She laughed. She enjoyed seeing me suffer[2].

As I walked home later I felt more ashamed than ever of my home, my job—of everything.

Time passed. I continued to work in the forge with Joe. Once a year on my birthday I went to visit Miss Havisham. I hoped to see Estella but I always returned home disappointed.

One night someone attacked[3] Mrs Joe. She couldn't walk or talk after that, so Biddy, a girl from the village, came to look after[4] us. She was a nice girl and clever too.

Then something happened that changed my life.

It was Saturday evening and Joe and I were in the Blue Boar Inn when a tall, dark man came in. He was well-dressed like a man from the city.

"Is there anyone here called Pip?" he asked the innkeeper[5].

"I'm Pip," I said.

He turned and looked at me carefully before saying. "I'd like to speak to you privately[6]. I have something important to tell you. Can we go to your house?"

---

1 abroad [ə'brɔd] (adv.) 在國外
2 suffer ['sʌfɚ] (v.) 受苦
3 attack [ə'tæk] (v.) 攻擊
4 look after 照顧
5 innkeeper ['ɪn,kipɚ] (n.) 旅館或餐館老闆
6 privately ['praɪvɪtlɪ] (adv.) 私下地

We walked back in silence. Joe opened the parlor[1] door and we sat around the table.

"My name is Jaggers," the man said. "And I'm a lawyer from London. I have a client[2] who is interested in your future, Pip. I must tell you that you have great expectations[3]!"

Joe and I looked at each other in great surprise. What did he mean?

"My client, your benefactor[4]," he continued, "wants you to be educated as a gentleman. You will receive a large sum[5] of money for this in the future."

My heart started beating wildly. "It must be Miss Havisham!" I thought.

"However, there are some conditions," the lawyer went on. "First you must leave the village immediately and go to London. You must never try to find out the name of your benefactor, and you must always be known as Pip. Do you accept these conditions?"

"Yes," I managed to say.

"Good!" said Mr Jaggers. "You'll need a tutor[6] and lodgings[7] in London. I know a man who can help you. His name is Pocket. Matthew Pocket."

---

1 parlor [ˈpɑrlɚ] (n.) 客廳；接待室
2 client [ˈklaɪənt] (n.) 委託人；客戶
3 expectations [ˌɛkspɛkˈteʃənz] (n.)
   〔複〕前程
4 benefactor [ˈbɛnəˌfæktɚ] (n.) 捐助人
5 sum [sʌm] (n.) 總數
6 tutor [ˈtjutɚ] (n.) 家庭教
7 lodgings [ˈlɑdʒɪŋz] (n.)
   〔複〕租住的房間
8 smart [smɑrt] (a.) 時髦的；瀟灑的
9 adopt [əˈdɑpt] (v.) 收養
10 guardian [ˈgɑrdɪən] (n.) 監護人

[25]   That evening Joe told Biddy about my good fortune. They were both very happy for me, but I knew that Joe was sad too. He didn't want to lose me. I was glad that Biddy was there to keep him and Mrs Joe company.

I spent my last few days in the town because I wanted to have some new clothes made. When they were ready, I put them on and went to see Miss Havisham.

As before, Miss Sarah Pocket came to open the gate when I rang. She was very surprised to see me.

"I'm going away and I'd like to say goodbye to Miss Havisham," I explained.

I climbed the stairs to her room and found her sitting near the table as usual.

"You look very smart[8], Pip," she said when she saw me.

"I'm going to London," I said. "I have been very lucky since I last saw you."

"Has a rich person adopted[9] you?"

"Yes," I replied. "And I'm very grateful."

"And is Mr Jaggers your guardian[10]?"

"That's right, Miss Havisham."

"Well!" she said. "You have a bright future in front of you. Be good and do what Mr Jaggers tells you. Goodbye, Pip! You'll always keep the name of Pip, you know."

The following morning Biddy called me at five o'clock. After a quick breakfast, it was time for me to leave. Joe and Biddy stood outside the forge and waved as I walked up the road. Suddenly I felt very sad and I almost turned round and went back.

I arrived in London about midday. Mr Jaggers' office was in Little Britain, which wasn't far from the coach[1] stop, so I decided to walk there. My first impression of the city was not very good—the streets were small, dirty and very crowded. The air was bad and everything was covered in dust.

A clerk[2] informed me that Mr Jaggers was still in Court[3].

"He'll be back soon," he said. "Please wait in here."

Mr Jaggers' office was not a very cheerful place, so I decided to go out and have a look around.

As I walked along a small side street, I passed Newgate Prison where the Courts were. There were small groups of people standing outside and I heard Mr Jaggers' name mentioned more than once. Behind the prison walls I could see the great dark dome[4] of Saint Paul's Cathedral[5].

Just before I got back to the office, I saw my guardian coming across the road towards me.

1 coach [kotʃ] (n.)（舊時的）四輪大馬車
2 clerk [klɜk] (n.) 辦事員
3 court [kort] (n.) 法院
4 dome [dom] (n.) 圓屋頂
5 cathedral [kəˈθidrəl] (n.) 大教堂

"Ah, Pip!" he said. "You're going to stay with young Mr Pocket at Barnard's Inn for a couple of[1] nights. On Monday he'll take you to his father's house. I have to go back to Court now, but Wemmick my clerk will look after you."

Barnard's Inn was a very shabby[2] building. Wemmick took me to the top floor and left me outside Mr Pocket's rooms. There was a notice on his door that said "Back soon," so I had to wait. Half an hour later I heard footsteps on the stairs and a young man appeared. He was about the same as age as me and he was carrying some strawberries.

"I'm very sorry," he said with a smile. "I'm late. I went to Covent Garden market to get some fruit for you. Here! Can you hold these strawberries while I open the door?"

1　a couple of 兩三個
2　shabby [ˈʃæbɪ] (a.) 破落的；寒酸的
3　goodness me 天哪

6. Life in London

The young man pushed and pulled the door and finally managed to open it.

"Please come in," he said. "I'm sorry there isn't much furniture, but I hope you'll be comfortable here until Monday. I don't earn very much and my father doesn't have much money to give me. Anyway, this is the sitting room and our bedrooms are over there. Oh, sorry! You're still holding the strawberries. Let me take them."

As I gave him back the fruit, we looked at each other.

"Goodness me[3]!" he said. "You're the boy from Satis House!"

"And you're the pale young gentleman!"

We both started laughing.

"Well, what a surprise!" he said shaking my hand kindly.

29 I liked Herbert Pocket (because Herbert was the young gentleman's name) immediately. He was an easy-going[1], cheerful[2] person, and very open[3].

That evening after dinner I asked him to tell me the story of Miss Havisham's life.

"Miss Havisham's mother died when she was a baby," he said. "After that her father gave her everything she wanted. Mr Havisham was very rich and very proud. His daughter was too."

"Was she an only child?" I asked.

"No, she wasn't. Her father married again, but secretly. I think the woman was a cook[4]. Anyway they had a son. A few years later when this wife died, Mr Havisham decided to tell his daughter about the secret marriage and her half-brother[5]. The boy became part of the family after that. However, he didn't turn out well[6] and finally his father sent him away.

"As a result[7], when Mr Havisham died, he left most of his money to his daughter. Her half-brother never forgave her for that."

"What happened then?"

1 easy-going [ˈizɪˌɡoɪŋ] (a.) 隨和的
2 cheerful [ˈtʃɪrfəl] (a.) 使人感到愉快的
3 open [ˈopən] (a.) 開放的
4 cook [kʊk] (n.) 廚子
5 half-brother [ˈhæfˌbrʌðɚ] (n.) 同父異母或同母異父的兄弟
6 turn out well 轉好
7 as a result 結果

"Well, not long after that, a man started to pay a lot of attention to[1] Miss Havisham. He followed her everywhere telling her how much he loved her. She believed him and soon she was deeply in love with him. When he asked her to marry him, she accepted. My father never trusted this man because he often asked Miss Havisham for large sums of money. That wasn't how real gentlemen behaved, he said. However, when my father told her to be careful, she became very angry. She ordered him to leave the house and never come back. Anyway, the day of the marriage was arranged, the wedding dress was bought, and the wedding invitations were sent. The day arrived, but not the bridegroom[2]. Instead he wrote her a letter . . . "

" . . . that she received," I said finishing his sentence, "while she was dressing for her wedding."

"At twenty minutes to nine," said Herbert. "Afterwards she stopped all the clocks in the house at that time."

"And she hasn't left the house since then," I said. "Is that all the story?"

"It's all I know," replied Herbert.

1   pay attention to . . . 注意到……
2   bridegroom [ˈbraɪdˌɡrʊm] (n.) 新郎
3   shrug [ʃrʌɡ] (v.) (n.) 聳肩
4   untidy [ʌnˈtaɪdɪ] (a.) 凌亂的
5   expression [ɪkˈsprɛʃən] (n.) 表情
6   remind someone of something
     使某人想起某事
7   lodger [ˈlɑdʒɚ] (n.) 寄宿人；房客

MISS HAVISHAM

- What did the bridegroom say in his letter to Miss Havisham?

- How did that event change Miss Havisham's life?

- How do you think she felt about men after that?

"Is this man alive now?"

"I don't know."

"What about Estella?"

Herbert shrugged[3] his shoulders. "Miss Havisham adopted her. I don't know any more than that. And now, my friend, you know as much about Miss Havisham as I do."

On Monday morning Herbert took me to his father's house in Hammersmith. Mr Matthew Pocket was a young-looking man with gray, untidy[4] hair and a worried expression[5].

"I'm glad to see you," he said with a smile that reminded me of[6] Herbert. "Please come with me. Your room is upstairs. I hope you'll like it."

I did. It was very pleasant and it had a view of the garden. Then Mr Pocket introduced me to his other lodgers[7]—two young men called Drummle and Startop. They had rooms on the same floor and they were also studying with Mr Pocket.

During the next few days we got to know each other quite well. Drummle was from a rich family in the south-west of England. He was large, arrogant[1], slow and lazy. Startop was just the opposite. Naturally I preferred his company to Drummle's.

Two or three days later Mr Pocket and I had a long talk. He gave me a lot of good advice about where to go in London and where to buy the things I needed. He was very kind and patient[2] and I was sure that I could learn a lot from him.

Although my room in Hammersmith was very comfortable, I decided to ask Mr Jaggers if I could keep my room at Barnard's Inn. I enjoyed spending time with Herbert and we were now good friends.

"You'll need to buy some furniture," my guardian said. "How much do you want? Five pounds[3]? Twice five? Four times five?"

"Twenty pounds will be more than enough," I replied.

"Wemmick! Give Mr Pip twenty pounds!" Mr Jaggers said opening the office door.

The clerk was sitting at his desk eating dry biscuits. He was putting them in his mouth like someone posting[4] letters in a letter box. Although he didn't say much when Mr Jaggers was there, he was a very friendly and warm person.

1 arrogant [ˋærəgənt] (a.) 傲慢的；自大的
2 patient [ˋpeʃənt] (a.) 耐心的
3 pound [paʊnd] (n.) 英鎊
4 post [post] (v.) 投郵

52 *Great Expectations*

That day he offered to show me around. While we were looking at some plaster[1] heads of murderers in Mr Jaggers' office, we talked about his employer[2].

"Has he invited you to have dinner with him yet?" Wemmick asked.

"No."

"Well, he will soon," he said. "He's going to invite your three friends too. There won't be a great variety of[3] food, but everything he gives you will be of the best quality. You can be sure of that. And when you're there, have a good look at his housekeeper[4]!"

"Why?" I asked. I was curious. "Will I see something strange?"

"A wild animal tamed[5]!"

I didn't have to wait long to satisfy my curiosity about Mr Jaggers' housekeeper. The dinner invitation arrived the next time I went to see my guardian.

"Meet me here," he said. Then he added, "And bring your friends!"

Mr Jaggers' house was in Soho. He lived in three dark rooms on the first floor. When we arrived, the table was already laid[6] for dinner in the best room.

---

1 plaster ['plæstɚ] (n.) 灰漿
2 employer [ɪm'plɔɪɚ] (n.) 雇主
3 a variety of 各種各樣的
4 housekeeper ['haʊsˌkipɚ] (n.) 女管家
5 tamed [temd] (a.) 馴服的
6 lay [le] (v.) 置放
   （三態：lay; laid; laid）
7 observe [əb'zɝv] (v.) 注意到；觀察
8 witch [wɪtʃ] (n.) 女巫
9 scar [skɑr] (n.) 疤；傷痕

We sat down and the housekeeper brought in the first dish. I observed[7] her closely. She was about forty years old and had long untidy hair. She reminded me of the witches[8] in Shakespeare's *Macbeth*.

While she was taking away the plates at the end of the meal, Mr Jaggers suddenly took hold of her hand.

"Show them your wrists, Molly," he said.

"Master!" she said in a low voice. "Please!"

He repeated his order and Molly turned over her hands to show us her wrists. There were deep scars[9] on one.

"These are strong wrists, gentlemen," said Mr Jaggers. "There's strength in these hands too. I've seen many hands in my time and I've never seen stronger—men's or women's. Thank you, Molly. You may go now."

Mr Jaggers sent us home at half past nine exactly. About a month later Drummle finished his studies with Mr Pocket and went back to his family. I can't say that I was sad to see him go. I don't think Startop was either.

7. Changes

One Monday morning I received a letter. It was from Biddy. It said:

My dear Mr Pip,

Mr Gargery has asked me to write to you to let you know that he is going to London and would like to see you. He will come to Barnard's Inn on Tuesday morning at nine o'clock. Your poor sister is much the same as when you left. We talk about you every night, and wonder what you are saying and doing. That's all, dear Mr Pip.

From,
Biddy

I am ashamed to say that I wasn't happy to receive this news. I didn't want to see Joe. I didn't want him to disturb my new life. He didn't belong in it. But there was no time to write and tell him not to come.

That evening I came into London from Hammersmith to be ready for him. The next morning I made sure that the sitting-room looked its best and that breakfast was on the table. Just before nine o'clock I heard Joe on the stairs. He waited outside the door for a long time before he finally knocked. I went to let him in.

"Joe! How are you, Joe?"

"Pip!" he replied. "How are you, Pip?"

His good honest face looked so happy as he shook my hand hard.

"I'm glad to see you, Joe. How are things at the forge?"

He was telling me about Mrs Joe and Biddy when a look of fear suddenly appeared on his face. I turned round and saw Herbert standing at his bedroom door. For no reason I felt annoyed[1] with poor Joe.

I introduced him to my friend and we sat down at the table to have breakfast. Joe clearly felt very uncomfortable with us. He didn't know what to say and was continually dropping[2] his food on the floor. His embarrassment only made me more embarrassed and I didn't do anything to help him.

1　annoyed [ə`nɔɪd] (a.) 心煩的
2　drop [drɑp] (v.) 掉落

It was very unkind of me, I know. I was glad when Herbert left and we were alone again. Then he told me the reason for his visit.

"I saw Miss Havisham, Pip. Miss Estella has come home and would like to see you."

I felt my face turn red as Joe finished delivering[1] his message.

"That's what I came to say, Pip, and now I'm going back home," he said standing up and putting his hat on.

"Aren't you going to stay for dinner?" I asked.

"No, Pip," he said. "I don't feel right here, in these clothes. I belong in the forge and the kitchen. On the marshes. Goodbye, Pip."

Then he touched me kindly on my face and left.

FEELING OUT OF PLACE

- Work with a friend. Think of some situations where you might feel out of place. Explain why.

- Talk about your own experiences of feeling out of place.

1 deliver [dɪˋlɪvɚ] (v.) 發表；講

The following day I got up early and bought a ticket for the coach. During the journey I thought about where to stay. "I should go to the forge," I thought, but then I began to invent many reasons for staying in the town instead. So, when I arrived, I went straight to the Blue Boar Inn.

The next morning I walked to Satis House. Miss Havisham was waiting for me. There was an elegant[1] lady sitting next to her. I couldn't see her face because she was looking down.

"Come in, Pip!" Miss Havisham said. "How are you?"

"I heard you wanted to see me, Miss Havisham, so I came immediately."

"Well?" she said. Her eyes moved to the lady near her.

The woman looked up. Then I saw that it was Estella. But a different Estella from the one I knew! She was no longer a proud young girl. She was a beautiful woman. She gave me her hand and I kissed it. Suddenly I felt like a clumsy village boy again.

"Has she changed?" asked Miss Havisham.

I could see that she was enjoying my embarrassment. "I didn't recognize her when I came in," I replied. "But now I can see the old . . . "

"What?" said Miss Havisham. "You aren't going to say the old Estella? She was proud and unkind!"

---

1 elegant [ˋɛləgənt] (a.) 優雅的

"And has he changed?" she asked Estella.

"Very much," replied the young lady looking at me and smiling.

"Less rough?"

Estella laughed.

As we sat there and talked, I found it difficult to separate[1] the past from the present. Seeing her again reminded me of my old dreams about being rich and living the life of a gentleman—the same dreams that made me feel ashamed of Joe and the forge. I realized then that Estella was part of me—part of my life.

Miss Havisham asked me to stay and have dinner.

"You can go back to town this evening," she said, "and catch the coach to London tomorrow."

Then to my surprise she said, "Mr Jaggers will be here soon because we have some business to discuss. You two can go into the garden for an hour."

As we walked along the path in the neglected[2] garden, Estella said, "I remember watching you fight here. Perhaps I'm a little strange, but I enjoyed it."

"Herbert and I are great friends now."

"Are you? Someone told me you were studying with his father."

I could still feel the differences between us as I walked next to her. She was very sure of herself and of her position[3] in life. I was like her servant.

"Do you remember the first day I came?" I asked. "You made me cry."

"No, I don't remember," she replied.

"But you must remember!"

"No," she said. "I don't. You must know that I have no heart. Perhaps that has something to do with my memory."

"But someone as beautiful as you must have a heart," I said, but I knew that it was a silly thing to say.

"Oh! Of course I have a heart that can be stabbed[4] or shot," said Estella. "And if it stops beating, I'll die. But you know what I mean. I have no softness, no sympathy[5], no feelings."

She looked at me and for a second I remembered another face. It must be Miss Havisham's, I thought. But, no, it wasn't hers. Then whose? I didn't know.

We walked around the garden a little longer; then we went back inside.

Miss Havisham was in the room with the long table. I stayed with her while Estella went to her room to get ready for dinner.

---

1   separate ['sɛpə,ret] (v.) 分開
2   neglected [nɪg'lɛktɪd] (a.) 棄置的
3   position [pə'zɪʃən] (n.) 地位
4   stab [stæb] (v.) 刺；刺傷
5   sympathy ['sɪmpəθɪ] (n.) 同情

"Is she beautiful?" she asked me. "Do you admire[1] her?"

"It's impossible not to," I replied.

Then she pulled me close to her and said with great passion, "Love her! Love her! If she likes you, love her! If she hurts you, love her! If she breaks your heart into pieces, love her! I adopted her to be loved, Pip."

She pulled me closer. "Do you know what love is?" she whispered. "Love means giving away your heart, like I did!"

Then she suddenly stood up and gave a wild cry. At that moment I heard the door close. I turned and saw my guardian standing in the room. Miss Havisham immediately sat down and became quiet again. She seemed a little embarrassed.

"You are very punctual[2], Jaggers!" she said. "Go with Pip and have dinner now."

While we were walking to the kitchen, Mr Jaggers told me that Miss Havisham never allowed anyone to see her eating or drinking.

"She walks around at night and eat and drinks what she finds," he said.

"May I ask you a question, Mr Jaggers?"

"You may, but I might refuse to answer it."

"Is Estella's name Havisham?"

"It is."

---

1 admire [əd`maɪr] (v.) 欣賞
2 punctual [`pʌŋktʃuəl] (a.) 守時的

After dinner Estella and I played cards for a while before Mr Jaggers and I returned to the Blue Boar. As I lay in bed that night I kept remembering Miss Havisham's words, "Love her! Love her!"

"I love her! I love her!" I repeated a hundred times to my pillow. "One day I will wake her sleeping heart," I thought happily. "But when will it be?"

The next day Mr Jaggers and I caught the coach and returned to London.

PIP AND ESTELLA

- Do Pip and Estella have anything in common?
- In what ways are they different?
- What must Pip do to wake Estella's "sleeping heart?"

Soon after my visit to Satis House a letter arrived for me. I didn't recognize the handwriting[1] on the envelope but I guessed who it belonged to. I opened it and read:

> I am arriving in London tomorrow.
> I believe that you agreed with Miss
> Havisham to meet me at the coach station.
> Miss Havisham sends her regards.
>
> Yours,
> Estella

The next day I went to the coach station hours before her coach arrived. When I finally saw her getting off, I thought that she looked more beautiful than ever.

"I'm going to Richmond," she told me. "You must take me there in a coach. Miss Havisham has given me the money for it. Here it is! We must obey her instructions, Pip. We aren't free to decide—you and I!"

I went and found a coach and we set off. When we passed through Hammersmith, I showed her where Mr Pocket lived.

[1] handwriting ['hænd,raɪtɪŋ] (n.) 筆跡

"It's quite near Richmond," I said. "I hope to see you sometimes."

"Oh, yes, you have to come," she said. "The family has already been told about you."

The journey was short and the time passed too quickly. A few minutes later we arrived at our destination[1] and Estella disappeared inside the house. I stood for a while looking at it and thinking. Although I wanted to live with her forever in that house, I knew that I was always miserable[2] when I was with her.

1 destination [ˌdɛstəˈneʃən] (n.) 目的地
2 miserable [ˈmɪzərəbl̩] (a.) 悲哀的
3 used to 過去習慣於
4 debt [dɛt] (n.) 債
5 bill [bɪl] (n.) 帳單
6 occasionally [əˈkeʒənlɪ] (adv.) 偶爾
7 funeral [ˈfjunərəl] (n.) 葬禮

8. A secret plan

45 I was now used to[3] the idea that I had great expectations and I spent as much money as I could. Herbert did too. As a result we both had large debts[4]. There were bills[5] everywhere in our rooms. Occasionally[6] we sat down together to put them in order. This made us feel better.

One evening, while we were admiring the tidy piles of bills in front of us, a letter with a black edge arrived for me.

"Oh, dear!" said Herbert. "That looks like bad news."

The letter informed me that my sister was dead. I didn't have very good memories of her, but the news shocked me and I felt sad. I wrote to Joe immediately and told him to expect me the following Monday for the funeral[7].

He was sitting alone at one end of the kitchen when I got to the house.

"Dear Joe," I said. "How are you?"

He took my hand. He was too upset to say anything.

My sister was buried in the churchyard next to our parents. Afterwards Uncle Pumblechook and some of the neighbors came back to the forge for something to eat. When Joe, Biddy and I were finally alone, Joe took off the big black cloak he was wearing and we sat in the parlor for a while. Nobody said very much.

Later Joe and I went into the forge. We talked about unimportant things and he began to relax. He was very pleased when I asked him if I could sleep in my old room that night.

Joe was already working in the forge when I went to say goodbye to him early the next morning. I promised to come and see him soon and often.

"Never too soon, Pip," he said "and never too often."

As I walked away, I thought about my promise. Did I intend[1] to keep it? I didn't think so.

The weeks passed and Herbert and I continued to spend lots of money and do nothing about our debts.

The day before my twenty-first birthday I received a note from Wemmick. He asked me to go to Mr Jaggers' office the following day. I didn't know what to expect.

"Well, Pip," Mr Jaggers said, "I must call you Mr Pip today. Congratulations, Mr Pip!"

---

1 intend [ɪnˋtɛnd] (v.) 想要；打算

We shook hands and I thanked him.

"Now, my young friend," my guardian began. "Is there anything you'd like to ask me?"

"Are you going to tell me the name of my benefactor today?"

"No. Ask another."

"Will you tell me soon?"

"I can't answer that," said Mr Jaggers. "Ask another."

I looked around me. I felt embarrassed, but there was one question I had to ask him.

"Am I going to receive anything, sir?"

"I was waiting for you to ask that question!" he said happily. He called Wemmick and told him to bring his book of accounts[1].

"Wemmick has written your name many times in his book," he said. "You are in debt I suppose. Am I right?"

"I'm afraid so, sir."

"Take this," he said giving me a piece of paper. "Now, look at it and tell me what it is."

"It's a banknote[2]," I replied. "For five hundred pounds."

"It is a present to you on your birthday," Mr Jaggers said. "Every year you'll receive the same sum of money. I'll be responsible for giving it to you until your benefactor chooses to appear. Goodbye, Pip."

1 account [ə'kaunt] (n.) 帳目
2 banknote ['bæŋknot] (n.) 鈔票

I stopped to talk to Wemmick on my way out. I had an idea in my head and I needed his advice.

"Mr Wemmick," I said. "I want to ask your opinion. I'd like to help a friend."

Then I told him about Herbert. I explained that I felt sorry for him. He was a very good person and a kind friend.

"My friend," I continued, "would like to work in business. But he's finding it difficult to get started because he has no money. I have money now, so I want to help him. Have you got any ideas about what I could do?"

Wemmick was silent for a while, and then he said, "That's very kind of you, Mr Pip. I know someone who might be able to help. I'll talk to him."

A week later a note arrived from Wemmick asking me to go and see him.

"Good news, Mr Pip!" he said. "My friend knows a young merchant[1] called Clarriker. He's just started a small company. He's looking for someone to invest in it and become his partner."

It sounded perfect for Herbert. I didn't want him to know what I was doing, so I went to see Wemmick's friend and we arranged everything secretly.

I'll never forget Herbert's happy face the day he told me that he was Mr Clarriker's partner. That night I cried when I was in bed. I was finally doing something good with my money.

PIP'S EXPECTATIONS

- Work with a partner. Discuss the questions. How did Pip's expectations change his life?
- How did they change him as a person?

After Estella arrived in London I spent most of my time in Richmond. I wasn't her only admirer—she had many—but only I was allowed to call her by her name. This, however, didn't mean that she thought more of me. She treated me badly because she knew that I was in love with her. But, although I never had one hour's happiness in her company, I never stopped wanting to be with her.

One evening we went to a ball in Richmond. I was surprised to see Drummle there. He didn't take his eyes off Estella, and she seemed to enjoy his attention.

"Why are you encouraging that man over there, Estella?" I said. "He isn't a good sort of person. Nobody likes him."

"I'm not encouraging[1] him!" she replied.

"You are," I said. "You never smile at me as much as you smile at him."

She turned and looked at me angrily.

"Do you want me to deceive[2] and trick[3] you?"

"Do you deceive and trick him, Estella?"

"Yes, and many others. All of them, except you. But I won't say any more."

---

1 encourage [ɪnˈkɜˈɪdʒ] (v.) 鼓勵
2 deceive [dɪˈsiv] (v.) 欺騙
3 trick [trɪk] (v.) 哄騙
4 take another direction
   轉了另一個方向
5 on business 出差
6 blow [blo] (v.) 吹
   (三態：blow; blew; blown)
7 footstep [ˈfʊtˌstɛp] (n.) 腳步聲

9. An unwelcome visitor

I was twenty-three years old when one night my life took another direction[4].

Herbert and I were now living on the top floor of a house near the river. I was alone that night because Herbert was in France on business[5]. I was listening to the wind blowing[6] down the river when suddenly I heard footsteps[7] on the stairs.

I picked up the lamp and went out to see who it was.

"Is there someone there?" I called.

"Yes," said a voice from the darkness below.

"Which floor do you want?"

"The top one, Mr Pip."

I held my lamp over the stairs. It lit up a man's face. I didn't recognize it, but the expression on it showed that the owner was pleased to see me.

He was dressed warmly but not elegantly. He had long gray hair and his skin was brown from spending a lot of time outside. I guessed he was about sixty.

"Do you want to see me?" I asked.

"Yes," he replied. "I do, master."

I took him inside. He looked around the room and smiled at what he saw. Then he did something strange. He held both of his hands out to me.

"What do you want?" I asked stepping back. I thought he might be mad[1].

He looked confused[2] and pushed his hands through his hair.

"Give me a minute to rest and I'll tell you," he replied.

He sat down in a chair near the fire. Suddenly I knew who he was! The convict in the churchyard!

He saw the change in my expression and came up to me holding his hands out again. This time I took them in mine. He kissed them and kept hold of[3] them.

"You helped me, Pip," he said. "I have never forgotten it."

He looked at me with great affection[4], but I could feel none for him. I took my hands away from his saying, "If you've come here to thank me, it isn't necessary. You must understand . . . "

"Understand what, Pip?"

"That my life has changed. I can't be your friend now. But you are wet and tired. Would you like something to drink before you go?"

"Thank you," he said slowly, not taking his eyes off[5] me.

---

1 mad [mæd] (a.) 發瘋的
2 confused [kənˈfjuzd] (a.) 困惑的
3 keep hold of 握緊

4 affection [əˈfɛkʃən] (n.) 情感
5 take one's eyes off . . .
　　把目光從……移開

I poured two drinks, one for him and another for myself. When I gave him his glass, I saw with amazement[1] that his eyes were full of tears.

"I'm sorry if my words hurt you," I said. "I didn't mean to be rude[2]."

As I put my glass to my lips, he held out his hand. I gave him mine, and then he drank.

THE UNWELCOME VISITOR

- How was Pip's visitor feeling?
- What were his expectations of Pip?

"What work do you do?" I asked him.

"I've been in Australia," he replied. "I worked as a sheep farmer there."

"I hope you have done well?"

"I've done very well."

"I'm glad to hear it."

Then he said with a smile, "May I ask you how you have done so well since we last met on the marshes?"

"I have a benefactor," I replied, a little embarrassed.

"Can I ask who?"

---

1 amazement [əˈmezmənt] (n.) 吃驚；驚異
2 rude [rud] (a.) 粗魯的
3 hesitate [ˈhɛzəˌtet] (v.) 猶豫
4 income [ˈɪnˌkʌm] (n.) 收入
5 figure [ˈfɪgjɚ] (n.) 數字

I hesitated[3] before saying, "I don't know the person's name."

"Could I guess what your income[4] is?" said the convict still smiling. "Is the first figure[5] five?"

My heart started to beat very fast.

"And do you have a guardian? A lawyer perhaps? And does his name begin with the letter 'J'?"

54 Suddenly I understood why he was there. I stood up and held the back of the chair. I couldn't speak or breathe[1]. The room began to turn. He caught me as I fell and carried me to the sofa.

"Yes, Pip," he said bringing his face close to mine. "It was me. I made you a gentleman. Didn't you ever think it was me?"

"No, never," I whispered.

"You're like a son to me, Pip," he went on. "When I was sent to the other side of the world, I thought about you all the time[2]. I worked hard for many years. Then my master gave me my freedom and some money. I started to work for myself and I did very well."

Again he took my hands and kissed them. I felt sick with disgust[3] when he touched me. I couldn't forget that this man was a criminal[4].

"But I was working for you, Pip," he went on. "It made me happy to think that you were spending my money." He pointed to a ring on my finger. "Gold and diamonds! A gentleman's ring. And look at these lodgings!"

I smiled weakly and he continued talking. "I made up my mind[5] to come back one day and see you. It wasn't easy, Pip, for me to leave those parts. And it wasn't safe. But I was determined and finally I did it!"

---

1 breathe [bri ð] (v.) 呼吸
2 all the time 一直
3 disgust [dɪsˋgʌst] (n.) 厭惡
4 criminal [ˋkrɪmən!] (n.) 罪犯
5 make up one's mind 下定決心

55　I didn't know what to say. I was too confused.

"Yes," he said. "I did it, but I'm very tired. I've been on a ship for months."

"My friend Herbert is away at the moment[6]. You can sleep in his room," I said.

"He won't come back tomorrow, will he?"

"No. Not tomorrow."

"Because," he said, speaking quietly and putting a long finger on my chest, "we must be careful."

"Why?" I asked.

"I was sent away for life[7] for trying to kill a man," he said. "If they find me, they'll hang[8] me.

This made me feel worse than I already felt. I disliked this man and he was risking his life[9] just to be with me!

I took him to Herbert's room and gave him some clean clothes. Five minutes later he was asleep. I went and sat next to the dying[10] fire. I was too unhappy to sleep. I tried to think, but there was only confusion in my head.

After an hour or two the horrible[11] truth started to become clear. Miss Havisham wasn't interested in me or my future at all. And she had no plans for me and Estella. She was using us to take her revenge[12] on men!

6　at the moment 此刻
7　for life 終生
8　hang [hæŋ] (v.) 吊死
　（三態：hang; hanged; hanged）
9　risk one's life 冒生命危險
10　dying [ˈdaɪɪŋ] (a.) 快熄滅的
11　horrible [ˈhɔrəbl̩] (a.) 可怕的
12　revenge [rɪˈvɛndʒ] (n.) 報仇；報復

I eventually fell asleep and when I woke up the clocks were striking[1] five. I got up and looked in Herbert's room. The convict was still there.

"I can't hide him here for very long," I thought. "People will wonder who he is."

The room was cold and dark so I made a fire and waited for him to wake up.

Daylight was coming in through the windows when he appeared. Once again I felt disgust for the man.

"I don't know your name," I said trying not to look at him.

"My name is Magwitch. Abel Magwitch," he replied.

"How long are you planning to stay in England?"

"How long?" he repeated surprised. "I'm not going back. I've come to stay."

"You can't stay here," I said quickly. "My friend will be back in a couple of days. I'll find you lodgings."

He seemed happy with that, so I went out later and found him a place. We spent the next five days in the house because I was too afraid to let him go out. Then Herbert arrived home.

It is difficult to describe[2] my friend's surprise when I told him about Magwitch. But I could see from his face that he shared my dislike of the man.

We had dinner together and then I took my guest to his lodgings. When I arrived back, Herbert was waiting for me with open arms. How lucky I was to have a friend like him!

---

1 strike [straɪk] (v.) (鐘) 敲 (三態：
    strike; struck; struck, stricken)
2 describe [dɪˈskraɪb] (v.) 描述
3 violent [ˈvaɪələnt] (a.) 暴力的

FRIENDS

- Who are your best friends?
- What do you like best about them?

"What can I do?" I asked. "I don't want to accept any more of this man's money. But he might kill me if he finds out! He has a violent[3] character."

"The answer is clear, my friend," replied Herbert. "Magwitch must leave England."

"He'll refuse to go," I said. "He's too attached[4] to me."

"Then you will have to take him!" Herbert replied.

The next day Magwitch told us the story of his life.

"I don't know where I was born or who gave me my name. I've never had a home. When I was a young boy, I had to steal to survive[5]. I was caught and put in prison. After that I was always in and out of prison. One day I met a man called Compeyson. He looked and spoke like a gentleman, but he wasn't. When I told him I was looking for work, he asked me to be his partner. What was his business? Swindling[6] people! And he was good at it too. He made others, like me, do the hard work and he took all the money. He had no heart, that man. I was always working, always getting into danger. Even my wife . . . "

---

4 attached [əˈtætʃt] (a.) 依戀的 6 swindle [ˈswɪndl̩] (v.) 詐騙
5 survive [səˈvaɪv] (v.) 活下來

He stopped and looked confused for a few seconds.

"But you don't need to know about her. Anyway, eventually we were caught. At the trial[1] he blamed[2] me for everything. And because he was dressed in good clothes and spoke nicely, the judge believed him. He gave Compeyson seven years and me fourteen. 'I'll smash[3] your face for this,' I told Compeyson. We were put on the same prison ship, but I never saw him. One night I escaped. Compeyson did too, but I didn't know that at the time. You told me, Pip. Do you remember? Later I found him on the marshes and smashed his face. That's why I was sent away for life."

Herbert was writing on a book cover. He quietly pushed it towards me and I read:

Compeyson was the name of Miss Havisham's lover.

---

1 trial ['traɪəl] (n.) 審問
2 blame [blem] (v.) 責備
3 smash [smæʃ] (v.) 粉碎
4 have a favor to ask 有事相求

10. Danger!

I wanted to speak to Estella and Miss Havisham before I left the country. Herbert understood and kindly offered to look after Magwitch while I went to Satis House.

To my surprise, the first person I saw when the coach arrived at the Blue Boar was Drummle. I guessed immediately why he was there. We exchanged a few, not very friendly words and then he left.

I didn't stop to eat anything, but walked straight to Satis House. I had a favor to ask[4] Miss Havisham, and there was something I wanted to tell Estella.

Miss Havisham was in her room and Estella was sitting next to her. They were surprised to see me.

"What brings you here, Pip?" said Miss Havisham.

"Miss Havisham," I began. "You are wrong to think that the Pockets are only interested in your money. I have spent a lot of time with them and I can say that Mr Matthew Pocket is the kindest, most honest person I know. His son Herbert is my best friend."

Miss Havisham looked uncomfortable. "What do you want for them?" she asked.

"If you have some extra[1] money, you can do something useful and good for Herbert," I said. "I started helping him two years ago, but I'm not able to continue doing it. I can't tell you why."

Miss Havisham looked into the fire and then at me. "Anything else?" she asked.

"Estella," I said turning to her. "I love you. I have loved you since the day I saw you. I have no hope that you will ever be mine, but I wanted you to know."

"When you say you love me," said Estella, "I understand the words, but they don't touch my heart. I'm not interested in how you feel. I told you before."

"Estella, do you love Bentley Drummle?"

She looked at Miss Havisham and didn't reply immediately. Then she said, "I'm going to marry him."

"Estella, dearest Estella! Don't let Miss Havisham influence[2] you in this. Give yourself to a better man than Drummle. I can't bear[3] to think of you with that man."

"It is my decision[4], not my adopted mother's," she replied coldly. "Anyway you'll soon forget me."

"Never!" I cried passionately[5]. "You are part of me, Estella. It's true that you have hurt me, but I never want to forget you."

---

1 extra [ˈɛkstrə] (a.) 額外的
2 influence [ˈɪnfluəns] (n.) 影響
3 bear [bɛr] (v.) 忍受
   (三態：bear; bear; bear)

4 decision [dɪˈsɪʒən] (n.) 決定
5 passionately [ˈpæʃənɪtlɪ] (adv.) 激動地

Estella's face showed no emotion[1], but I saw a look of shock on Miss Havisham's face as I left the room.

EMOTIONS

- Work with a partner. What do people do when they feel _____
  - ☐ shocked?
  - ☐ scared?
  - ☐ excited?
  - ☐ angry?
- Make notes and share your ideas with the class.

I decided to walk back to London because I wanted to be alone with my unhappiness. It was after midnight when I finally arrived home. As I was going through the gate the guard stopped me.

"Someone left a note for you, sir," he said handing me a piece of paper.

I opened it and immediately recognized Wemmick's writing. "DON'T GO HOME!" the note said.

Why mustn't I go home? Was I in danger? Was Magwitch in danger? Suddenly I was afraid. I rushed back to the street, called a Hackney cab[2] and told the driver to take me to an inn in Covent Garden.

I slept very little and as soon as it was light I went to see Wemmick. He told me that someone was watching my house. My heart jumped. It must be Compeyson, I thought. He knows that Magwitch is here. He wants to kill him before Magwitch finds him. I could see that Wemmick understood my thoughts.

"I've advised Herbert," he continued, "to take your guest to a safer place. I believe he has taken him to his fiancée's[3] house."

Herbert's fiancée was called Clara. She lived near Greenwich. I decided to go there immediately.

Herbert opened the door and took me straight into the parlor.

"Clara's upstairs with her father," he said. "He's ill and can't move from his bed."

"What about Magwitch? Is he alright?" I asked anxiously[4].

"Yes, he's fine," Herbert replied. "But he'll be glad to see you. Come on!"

---

1 emotion [ɪ`moʃən] (n.) 情感
2 Hackney cab 出租馬車
3 fiancée [ˌfiən`se] (n.) 未婚妻
4 anxiously [`æŋkʃəslɪ] (adv.) 緊張不安地

I followed him upstairs to a small room on the top floor.
Magwitch was sitting by the fire looking calm and comfortable.
He was pleased to see me.

"Magwitch," I said. "Do you trust Mr Jaggers and Wemmick?"

"Oh, yes," he replied. "They know everything."

"Well, I saw Wemmick this morning. He had some bad news.
Someone knows you are here, Magwitch. It's too dangerous for
you to stay. You must leave the country as soon as possible."
Then I added quickly, "I'll come with you of course."

I expected him to refuse to go, but he understood that he was in danger.

"Pip, I have a plan," said Herbert. "You and I are both good boatmen[1]. We can take Magwitch down the river ourselves. We don't want other people to know about his escape, do we? You must get a boat immediately. If you start going up and down the river every day, people will get to know you. Then, when we leave with Magwitch, they won't be suspicious[2].

1 boatman ['botmən] (n.) 船夫
2 suspicious [sə'spɪʃəs] (a.) 可疑的

I liked Herbert's idea and Magwitch was happy with the plan too.

"Good! That's what we'll do then," I said. "Now I must go, Magwitch. You'll be safe here with Clara and Herbert."

"Dear boy," he answered, taking my hands. "I don't know when we'll meet again, and I don't like saying goodbye. So I'll say goodnight!"

"Goodnight! Herbert will be our messenger[1]."

He stood at the top of the stairs and watched us go down. My feelings at that moment surprised me. I was anxious and sad about leaving him. He no longer filled me with disgust.

"I've changed a lot since he first arrived here," I thought as I walked home.

The next day I got a boat. I began to go out on the river regularly, sometimes alone, sometimes with Herbert.

One evening after my exercise on the river, I met Mr Jaggers. He invited me to have dinner with him.

"Wemmick's coming too," he said.

He was already there when Mr Jaggers and I arrived. We sat down around the table and Molly started serving dinner immediately.

Just after we started to eat Mr Jaggers turned to Wemmick and said, "Did you give Pip that note from Miss Havisham?"

"No, sir. It's still in my pocket," replied the clerk. "Here it is!"

"It's just two lines, Pip," Mr Jaggers said. "Miss Havisham wants to discuss something with you. Business. She says you'll understand."

"I'll go tomorrow," I said hoping that the business involved[2] Herbert.

Molly came in and put another dish on the table. The movement[3] of her hands caught my attention. It reminded me of another pair of hands that moved in the same way. I looked at her more closely. Those eyes! I knew them well. Then suddenly it came to me. They were Estella's eyes!

On the way home I asked Wemmick to tell me about Molly.

"About twenty years ago, she was tried[4] for the murder of a woman," he said. "Mr Jaggers was her lawyer. He defended[5] her and won the case. Soon after that she started working for him. I believe she had a child. Some people say she killed it to get revenge on her husband."

"Was the child a boy or a girl?" I asked.

"A girl."

1 messenger [ˈmɛsn̩dʒɚ] (n.) 使者；信差
2 involve [ɪnˈvɑlv] (v.) 包含
3 movement [ˈmuvmənt] (n.) 動作
4 try [traɪ] (v.) 審判
5 defend [dɪˈfɛnd] (v.) 辯護

11. A journey down the river

Miss Havisham looked different when I saw her the following day. She was less proud and she seemed almost afraid of me.

"The last time you were here, Pip," she said, "you told me I could do something useful and good for your friend. What is it?"

I explained to her the secret history of how Herbert became a partner in Mr Clarriker's company.

"I hoped to complete the payments myself," I said, "but my situation has changed recently. Now I'm not able to finish the job I started."

"So?" she asked. "How much more money is needed?"

I was a little afraid of telling her. It seemed like a very large sum.

"Nine hundred pounds."

She stood up and went over to a writing table. A minute or two later she came back with a piece of paper.

"Give this to Mr Jaggers," she said. "He'll give you the money."

Before I could thank her, she added, "My name is at the bottom of that paper, Pip. If you can ever write under it 'I forgive[1] her,' please do it."

"Miss Havisham! I can do it now," I said. "I have also made mistakes in my life and need to be forgiven. How could I not forgive you?"

She took my hand and brought it to her face. She was crying.

"Oh! What have I done?" she sobbed[2].

I knew she was thinking about me and Estella.

When she was calmer[3] I asked, "Do you know who Estella's parents are, Miss Havisham?"

"No, Pip. Mr Jaggers brought her here."

I went straight back to London after my visit to Satis House. Herbert was at home when I got there.

"Is everything alright down the river?" I asked anxiously.

"Yes, fine," replied Herbert cheerfully. "I sat with Magwitch for two hours last night. He told me a lot more about his past. When he spoke to us before, he mentioned his wife. Do you remember?"

"Yes, I do," I said.

"Well, it seems that she was arrested and tried for the murder of a woman! Mr Jaggers was her lawyer. It was one of his first cases and he won it. It made him famous in London."

"What else?"

"She and Magwitch were together for about five years and they had a child. Perhaps he treated this woman badly, or perhaps not. Anyway on the night of the murder the child, a girl, disappeared. Magwitch was sure she was dead, killed by the mother to get her revenge on him."

---

1 forgive [fəˋgɪv] (v.) 寬恕
   （三態：forgive; forgave; forgiven）

2 sob [sɑb] (v.) 嗚咽；啜泣
3 calm [kɑm] (a.) 冷靜的

MAGWITCH

- Who do you think Magwitch's wife was?
- Do you think his child is dead?
- If not, what happened to her?

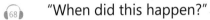

"When did this happen?"

"About three or four years before he met you. He said you reminded him of his little girl."

"Herbert!" I said. My voice was shaking with emotion now. "The man we are hiding in Clara's house is Estella's father!"

Early the next morning I went to see Mr Jaggers. He was surprised when I gave him the piece of paper from Miss Havisham.

"Wemmick!" he said. "Write a check[1] for nine hundred pounds and bring it to me to sign."

Before I left to go to Clarriker's, I told Mr Jaggers everything I knew about Estella's parents. Of course he knew that Molly was her mother, but he had no idea that Magwitch was her father.

A few weeks after this, I decided that it was time for me and Magwitch to leave. My plan was to row[2] down the river to Gravesend and take one of the steamers[3] that regularly left London for Hamburg. I planned our departure[4] for the following Wednesday.

When the day came, it was sunny, but there was a cold wind on the river. Herbert and I got into the boat and started rowing down to Greenwich. I felt happy to be doing something at last, and it was pleasant to be on the river in the spring sunshine.

"Is he there?" asked Herbert as we approached[5] Clara's house.

"Yes," I replied. "Slowly, Herbert! Pull on the oars[6]!"

The boat touched the side lightly for a single moment and Magwitch jumped on board. He was carrying a heavy coat and a black bag.

"Dear boy!" he said, putting his arm on my shoulder as he sat down. "Well done. Thank you!"

Nobody took any notice of us as we moved down the river. At first we passed lots of ships, but away from the city, the river became quieter and the countryside was flat[7]. The only noise was the cry of the seabirds.

We stopped once to rest and eat something, but we were soon back on the river. As the sun went down, it began to get colder. We needed to find somewhere to spend the night. Finally we saw a light on the river bank, so we stopped and tied up the boat.

1 check [ˋtʃɛk] (n.) 支票
2 row [ro] (v.) 划（船）
3 steamer [ˋstimɚ] (n.) 汽船
4 departure [dɪˋpartʃɚ] (n.) 離開
5 approach [əˋprotʃ] (v.) 接近
6 oar [or] (n.) 槳
7 flat [flæt] (a.) 平坦的

The light was coming from the window of an inn. We went inside and asked the innkeeper for rooms for the night. It was a small, dirty place, but there was a good fire in the kitchen and bacon and eggs to eat. After dinner I lay down without taking off my clothes and slept well for a few hours. When I woke up, the wind was blowing hard.

We set off early and at about half past one we saw the Hamburg steamer in the distance. It was coming towards us at full speed[1]. Magwitch and I picked up our bags and got ready to board it. As we were saying goodbye to Herbert, I noticed another boat near the river bank. It was also coming towards us. There were two men sitting at the front and four others rowing. One of the men sitting was steering[2] the boat. He was looking at us while the other one, wrapped[3] in a large coat, was whispering something to him.

I could hear the steamer getting closer and closer. The other boat was almost touching ours now. Suddenly the man who was steering it spoke to us.

THE OTHER BOAT

- Who could the men in the boat be?
- What are they going to do?

---

1 at full speed 全速
2 steer [stɪr] (v.) 掌舵
3 wrap [ræp] (v.) 包裹

"You have a returned convict there," he said. "His name is Abel Magwitch. I arrest that man!"

As he said this, he took hold of[1] our boat and put his hand on Magwitch's shoulder. This caused great confusion on board the steamer. I heard people calling to us, and then I heard the steamer stop.

1 take hold of 抓住
2 splash [splæʃ] (n.) 濺水聲

At the same moment, Magwitch jumped up and pulled the coat away from the other man in the front of the boat. I saw his face for only a second. It was the younger convict! Compeyson!

Then there was a loud cry from the steamer and a loud splash[2]. Our boat turned over and I was in the water. It all happened very quickly. Fortunately I was soon pulled on board the other boat with Herbert. I looked for Magwitch, but there was no sign of him or Compeyson in the water.

The four rowers pulled on their oars to stop the boat from turning over as the steamer moved away. Then, as they were rowing towards the river bank, we saw a dark shape in the water. It was Magwitch! We took hold of him and quickly pulled him on board. He had a deep cut on his head and another on his chest. We looked for Compeyson for a long time, but we never found him.

12. A new start

Magwitch was taken to a hospital in London. I was allowed to go with him and look after him during the journey. I held his hand and looked at him. I no longer saw a dangerous convict, but an affectionate[1], generous man—a better man than me.

His trial was arranged for the following month. He was too ill to go to prison, so he stayed in the hospital. Although I saw him every day, I never saw a change for the better in his condition.

One evening during this dark period of my life, Herbert came home and announced that Clarriker's was sending him to work in Egypt.

"It's a good opportunity," he said. "I must go." Then he added after a short pause[2], "Have you thought about your future, Pip?"

"No," I answered. "I'm too afraid to."

"Well," he said. "We'll need a clerk in the office in Cairo. What about coming with me?"

---

1 affectionate [əˈfɛkʃənɪt] (a.) 溫柔親切的
2 pause [pɔz] (n.) 暫停；中斷

"Thank you, Herbert," I said. "It's a very kind offer. But I'm afraid that I'm too worried at the moment to be able to make a decision. I'll think about it and let you know."

Magwitch was sentenced[1] to death at his trial. A few days later when I arrived to visit him, I saw that he was dying. I took his hand gently.

"My dear boy!" he managed to say. "You've never deserted[2] me."

I pressed[3] his hand. I remembered a time when I wanted to desert him.

"Are you in much pain today?" I asked.

"I can bear it, dear boy."

"Dear Magwitch, I must tell you something," I said. "Can you understand what I say?"

He pressed my hand.

"You had a child once. A child you loved and lost. Now she's a lady and she's very beautiful. And I love her!"

He lifted my hand to his lips. Then his head fell quietly on his chest.

After Magwitch died, I was ill for many weeks. I can remember only one thing from that time—Joe's face. He was there all the time, looking after me. One day when I was feeling better, I woke up and found a note on the table. It said:

> I have gone home, Pip, because you are well again and don't need old Joe.

There was also a receipt[4] for the payment of all my debts. That day I made two decisions. One was to go to the forge and thank Joe. The other was to ask Biddy to marry me.

PIP'S FUTURE

- **What do you think? Tick (✓) Yes or No.**
  1. Biddy will agree to marry Pip.
     ☐ Yes ☐ No
  2. Pip will go back to his job at the forge.
     ☐ Yes ☐ No
  3. Pip will never see Estella again.
     ☐ Yes ☐ No

---

1 sentence [ˋsɛntəns] (v.) 判刑
2 desert [dɪˋzɝt] (v.) 遺棄
3 press [prɛs] (v.) 壓
4 receipt [rɪˋsit] (n.) 收據

Biddy now taught at the village school, so I went there first. However, when I arrived it was closed. The forge was closed too. I found Joe and Biddy in the kitchen. They were both surprised to see me.

"But Joe! Biddy! How smart you are today!" I said.

Biddy looked at Joe and smiled.

"It's our wedding day, Pip," she said. "Joe and I are married!"

I had to sit down because I suddenly felt very weak. When I was feeling stronger, I was able to say, "Dear Biddy, you have the best husband in the world. And, dear Joe, you have the best wife in the world. You'll make each other very happy. And I want to thank both of you for all you have done for me. I have repaid[1] you badly for your kindness, I know."

Joe started to say something, but I stopped him and continued. "I'm going abroad to work soon. I intend to send you all the money I owe you, Joe. And now, although I know you have already done it in your own kind heart, please tell me that you forgive me!"

"Dear old Pip," said Joe with tears in his eyes. "There's nothing to forgive!"

We had dinner together, and afterwards Joe and Biddy came with me to the coach stop to say goodbye.

---

1 repay [rɪ'pe] (v.) 報答

When I got back to London, I sold everything I had and went to join Herbert in Egypt. I was there for eleven years. When I eventually returned to England, Joe and Biddy were the first people I went to see.

One evening I went to look at Satis House. It was beginning to get dark and there was already a pale moon in the sky. The house was now in very bad condition so I walked around the garden. I knew from Joe that Miss Havisham was dead. I also knew that Drummle was dead too.

As I remembered this, I saw a woman at the end of the garden path.

"Estella!"

"Pip! I'm surprised you recognize me!"

She looked older, but she was still beautiful.

We walked and talked for a while and then she said, "Tell me that we are still friends, Pip."

"We are friends," I replied.

I took her hand in mine and, as the moon rose higher in the sky, we left the garden together.

Ⓐ Personal Response

1 Answer the questions. Share your ideas with the rest of the class.

- [a] Did you enjoy reading the story?
- [b] Which character was the most interesting?
- [c] Would you recommend the story to any of your friends?
- [d] Did you learn anything about life in Victorian times (when Dickens was writing)?
- [e] Do you think the story could work with a modern setting?
- [f] Would you like to see a film version of the story?

2 Work in small groups. Make a list of films or stories you know in which _____

- [a] one of a pair of lovers is poor and the other is rich.
- [b] the main character is poor and then becomes rich.
- [c] the theme is revenge.

❸ Comprehension

3 Choose the correct answer.

_____ a Pip helped the convict in the churchyard because

⬚ 1 he was sorry for him.

⬚ 2 he was afraid of him.

_____ b Pip felt ashamed of his home and family because

⬚ 1 Estella was unkind.

⬚ 2 Miss Havisham was rude to him.

_____ c Miss Havisham wanted Pip to love Estella because

⬚ 1 it was part of a plan.

⬚ 2 Estella liked him.

_____ d In London Pip

⬚ 1 studied hard.

⬚ 2 spent a lot of money.

_____ e Magwitch had to leave England because Compeyson

⬚ 1 knew he was there.

⬚ 2 tried to kill him.

4 Read the sentence and tick (✓) true (T) or false (F).

T F   a) Pip's full name was Philip Gargery.

T F   b) Miss Havisham was engaged to Compeyson.

T F   c) Mr Matthew Pocket was Miss Havisham's favorite nephew.

T F   d) Mr Jaggers' housekeeper was Estella's mother.

5 Read these sentences from the story. Write the missing names and answer the questions about those characters.

a) _____ put on his leather apron and started work immediately. What did this character start doing?

b) _____ and _____ thought that Miss Havisham had plans for my future.
Why did these characters think this?

c) _____ was from a rich family in the south-west of England. What did this character do later in the story?

[d] One Monday morning I received a letter. It was from

_____.

How did this character surprise Pip later in the story?

[e] _____ eventually found Magwitch and led the
police to him.

Why did this character lead the police to Magwitch?

6 Work with a partner. Try to remember how these things
were involved in the story.

[a] a pork pie

[b] cards

[c] 25 guineas

[d] a letter with a black edge

[e] a boat

C Characters

7 Which adjective in the box best describes Pip as a child?
Write a sentence to explain your choice.

> ambitious   cruel   generous   hard-working
> kind   lucky   realistic   sensitive

8 Read the sentences about Pip as a young man in London.
Tick (✓) true (T) or false (F).

- T F [a] He missed Joe and his sister.
- T F [b] He spent more money than he had.
- T F [c] He studied law.
- T F [d] He got a job in an office.
- T F [e] He went to a ball with Estella.
- T F [f] Herbert was his best friend.
- T F [g] He frequently met Estella.
- T F [h] He sometimes went to the theater.

9 Answer the questions about Pip.

- [a] How did the relationship between Pip and Joe change after Pip went to London?
- [b] What was his relationship with Joe like at the end of the story?
- [c] Why did Pip feel disgust for Magwitch when the convict arrived at his lodgings?
- [d] Why did Pip's feelings about Magwitch change from dislike to admiration?

10 Which character does Pip describe as the following?

    a sweet-tempered and easy-going _____

    b bad-tempered and busy   _____

    c tall and dark   _____

    d easy-going and cheerful   _____

11 Answer the questions about Estella.

    a Choose two adjectives from the box to describe Estella. Write sentences to explain your choices.

> arrogant   honest   insensitive
> independent   rude   selfish

    b How does Estella win Pip's love?

    c Why does Estella marry Drummle?

    d How do you think her feelings towards Pip change when she finds out the identity of her parents?

12 Write a sentence about the relationship between the following pairs of characters.

    a Mrs Joe / Uncle Pumblechook

    b Miss Havisham / Estella

    c Joe / Biddy

    d Magwitch / Molly

    e Herbert / Clara

    f Mr Jaggers / Wemmick

13 Think of one good thing and one bad thing that Miss Havisham does.

14 What is your opinion of Magwitch? Is he a bad character or a good one? Give reasons for your answer.

D Plot and Theme

15 Put the events from the story into the correct order.

_____ (a) Pip became Joe's apprentice.

_____ (b) An escaped convict asked Pip to steal food and a file for him.

_____ (c) Magwitch arrived one night at Pip's lodgings.

_____ (d) Pip went to play at Satis House and met Estella.

_____ (e) Mr Jaggers told Pip he had great expectations.

_____ (f) Pip discovered the identity of Estella's parents.

_____ (g) Pip met Estella in the gardens of Satis House.

_____ (h) Pip received £500 on his 21st birthday.

_____ (i) Magwitch was caught while he was trying to leave the country.

_____ (j) Pip started his studies with Mr Matthew Pocket.

_____ (k) Pip went abroad to work.

_____ (l) Estella and Pip met in London.

16 Work with a partner or in a small group. Read the question and answer it for each statement ((a) (b) (c)).

Pip's moral and psychological development can be divided into three stages (see below). How does Pip change as he goes through those stages?

   ⒜ before he has a secret benefactor
   ⒝ in London as a gentleman
   ⒞ after he discovers Magwitch is his benefactor

Present your answers to the rest of the class.

17 When Pip discovers that Magwitch is his benefactor, he refuses to accept any more money from him. Why do you think he does this?

18 The last time that Pip goes to see Miss Havisham she asks him to forgive her? What for?

19 Match a theme in the story (a-e) with an event (①-⑤) that relates to it.

> a Crime   d Ambition
>
> b Wealth   e Revenge
>
> c Social class

_____ ① Pip dreamt of belonging to Miss Havisham's world and marrying Estella.

_____ ② Pip felt ashamed of Joe when they visited Miss Havisham.

_____ ③ Compeyson and Magwitch were arrested for swindling people.

_____ ④ Miss Havisham enjoyed watching Pip suffer when Estella was cruel to him.

_____ ⑤ Magwitch wanted to make Pip a gentleman with the money he earned.

20 Add another event from the story to each of the themes in Exercise **19**.

21 Complete the sentences in a suitable way.

a Estella was a proud and beautiful girl who _____

b Pip loved Estella although _____

c Pip wanted to help Herbert because _____

d Pip didn't want Herbert to know that he was helping him so _____

E Language

22 Match the adjectives a-e with the words 1-5 to make combinations from the story.

_____ a rough   1 ring
_____ b deep   2 fog
_____ c good   3 hands
_____ d iron   4 advice
_____ e thick   5 scars

23 Write a sentence for each of the combinations in Exercise **22**. Your sentences must relate to the story.

a _____

b _____

c _____

d _____

e _____

24 Underline the wrongly spelt word in the sentences. Write it correctly in the space.

a Joe was a blaksmith. _____

b Mrs Joe invited the neightbors to Christmas dinner.

_____

c There was a triumfant look on Estella's face.

_____

d Pip became Joe's aprentice. _____

25 Read the sentences and circle the correct word.

[a] Pip went to Satis House to thank Miss Havisham of / for helping him.

[b] Magwitch wanted to educate Pip to / as a gentleman.

[c] When Pip arrived at Mr Jaggers' house, the table was already laid / put for dinner.

[d] Joe was too / so upset at the funeral to talk to Pip.

26 Complete the sentences with the verbs in the box in the correct form.

> bring up   give away   go back
> set off   turn out   turn over

[a] Mrs Joe _____ Pip _____ because their parents were dead.

[b] "Love means _____ your heart like I did!" said Miss Havisham.

[c] Mr Havisham's son _____ to be bad.

[d] Mr Jaggers couldn't take Pip to Herbert's lodgings because he had to _____ to Court.

[e] Pip met Estella at the coach station and they _____ for Richmond immediately.

[f] Everyone in the boat fell in the water when it _____.

27 Put the words in the questions in the correct order.

a) Who / a / pie / beautiful / gave / Christmas / pork / for / Mrs Joe?

_____

b) What / in / covered / at / Satis House / cobwebs / was?

_____

c) Where / when / stay / first / did / arrived / Pip / he / in / London?

_____

d) How much / Mr Jaggers / his / did / Pip / give / on / 21st birthday?

_____

e) Why / Magwitch / take / Herbert / his / did / to / fiancée's / house?

_____

28 Work with a partner. Ask and answer the questions in Exercise **27**.

a) _____

b) _____

c) _____

d) _____

e) _____

TEST

1 Listen and tick (✓) the correct picture.

a

1

2

b

1

2

c

1

2

d

1

2

⭐ **2** Choose the correct answer.

_____ a How did Pip get his name?

1 His mother chose it.

2 It was his father's name.

3 He invented it himself.

4 It is a short form of his name.

_____ b How did Pip feel after his first visit to Satis House?

1 Angry. 3 Happy.

2 Ashamed. 4 Lucky.

_____ c How often did Pip return to his village after he moved to London?

1 Never. 3 Once a month.

2 A couple of times. 4 Regularly.

_____ d Why was Magwitch sent to Australia for life?

1 He tried to kill a man.

2 He tried to kill his wife.

3 He stole money from people.

4 He was poor and had no future.

_____ e How did Pip feel about Magwitch at the end of the story?

1 He was sorry for him. 3 He hated him.

2 He disliked him. 4 He was grateful to him.

PROJECT WORK

London in **Great Expectations**

1 Work in groups. Make a poster of a map of London, similar to this. Mark the following places mentioned in the story.

- ★ *Little Britain (a street in the City of London where Mr Jaggers' office is)*
- ★ *Newgate Prison (near Mr Jaggers' office)*
- ★ *St Paul's Cathedral (behind Newgate Prison)*
- ★ *Barnard's Inn (in Holburn where Pip and Herbert live)*
- ★ *Soho (where Mr Jaggers lives)*

2 Find an interesting fact about each place.
Write it in an information box next to the place.

3 Display your poster in the classroom.

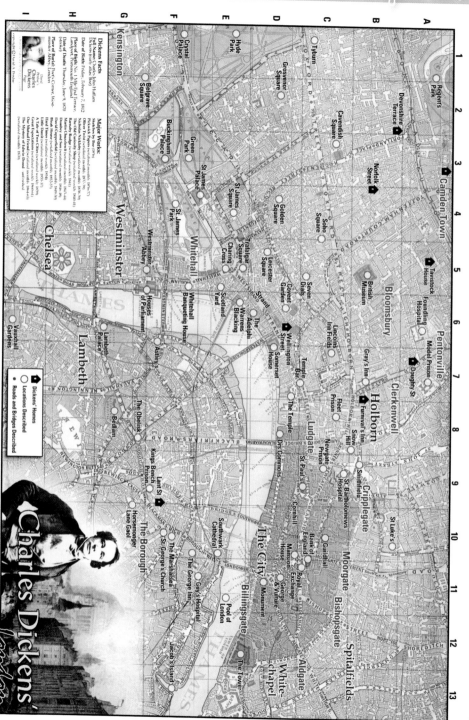

作者簡介

查爾斯・狄更斯於 1812 年 2 月 7 日出生於樸茨茅斯，在八個孩子中排行老二。父親約翰・狄更斯是海軍職員。1814 年，狄更斯一家搬到倫敦。兩年後，又遷居肯特的查塔姆。在 1822 年全家搬回倫敦前，查爾斯在當地上了幾年私立學校。

兩年後，父親因為欠債未還，被送進欠債監獄。查爾斯當時 12 歲。因為家裡沒錢，他只好休學到鞋油製造廠工作。那裡的條件很差，工人們都很貧窮。那是一個與查爾斯以往所認知的世界完全不同的地方，他常感到落寞悲傷。

在父親設法出獄後，查爾斯重回校園。然而，這次的經驗對他產生了莫大的影響，讓他永遠無法忘懷，也在好幾本小說內描述了類似的經歷。

15 歲時，他離開了學校，在法律事務所擔任職員。隨後，他又在法庭擔任記者。 1836 年，他的第一本小說《匹克威克外傳》出版，該書非常暢銷，他也展開了小説家的生涯。

查爾斯・狄更斯對英國古典文學有很大的貢獻，深受敬愛。他最著名的一些小說，包括《孤雛淚》（1837）、《小氣財神》（1843）、《塊肉餘生記》（1850）、《孤星血淚》（1860）等。

查爾斯・狄更斯於 1870 年辭世，長眠於倫敦西敏寺。

本書簡介

《孤星血淚》（又譯：遠大前程）常被歸為是「成長小說」（bildungsroman），在維多利亞時代，這是一種風行的小說形式。「bildungsroman」是德文，這類小說呈現角色在成長過程中的心理與道德發展歷程。不過，一如查爾斯・狄更斯的大多數小説一樣，《孤星血淚》也無法輕易地被定義歸類，因為這也是一個愛與激情的故事，也是一個懸疑故事，也是一部反應當時社會的小説。

《孤星血淚》的時空背景，設定於 1800 年代初期到中期，故事發生在肯特沼澤區和倫敦。主角是一位名叫皮普的可憐孤兒，他和姊姊、姊夫喬住在一起。有一天，他遇上了一個富家女艾絲黛拉，還愛上了對方，但對方嘲笑他是個鄉下窮小子。此後，他開始不滿自己的生活。

幾年後，他得知自己有個神祕的贊助人，希望他能過上紳士的生活。如今他有錢了，覺得自己有機會贏得艾絲黛拉的芳心。他離開村莊，來到倫敦，在那裡結交了新朋友。他開始為自己的出身和家人感到羞愧，特別是喬，他對待喬很苛刻。然而，在諸多歷練之後，他終於體認到自己所犯的錯誤。

這部小說的結局，查爾斯・狄更斯原本以悲劇收場，但由於一個朋友的建議，他決定讓結局以喜劇落幕。現在大多數的版本採用新結局，但仍有部分維持原案。

1. 墓地奇遇

P.15

　　我父親的姓是皮利普，我的名字叫菲利浦。這名字對小時候的我來說，很難唸，所以我乾脆說自己叫皮普。從那時候起，大家就叫我皮普了。

　　我的父母親雙雙過世，我和姊姊同住。她大我二十歲，嫁給了本地的鐵匠喬·葛吉利。喬是個老好人，很好相處，棕髮藍眼。姊姊喬·葛吉利太太，恰恰相反，她黑髮、黑眼睛，脾氣可壞了。她因為一刻也不得閒，洋裝上幾乎都是套上圍裙。我常感受到她強而有力的雙手，在我的頭旁邊揮動著，她對喬也是這樣，但喬都不吭一聲。我搞不懂他怎麼會娶我姊，我猜是我姊逼婚的。

　　我們住在沼澤邊的村莊裡。那裡的土地平坦，但因為靠海，植被不多，就一片蒼茫、刮風的荒野之地。

P.16

　　一個霧濛濛的傍晚，我找到了父母的墓地，那在離我們住的村莊約一英里遠的舊教堂那邊，半隱在墓園的漫漫長草裡。我看著基碑上的名字，菲利浦·皮利普，與愛妻喬治安娜。這一幕，令我心酸，我開始哭了起來。

　　突然，一個可怕的聲音大吼道：「安靜，不然就割斷你的喉嚨！」

　　我抬頭一看，見到霧中出現一個男人，向我走來。他沒戴帽子，一雙鞋又舊又破，衣衫襤褸，滿身泥巴，腳上套著一個大鐵環。

　　他用一隻手托住我的下巴。我很驚恐。

　　「噢，先生，不要割斷我的喉嚨！拜託，不要！」我哭叫著。

　　「你叫什麼名字？快說！」男人問。

　　「先生，皮普。」

　　「什麼？」那個男人把臉湊近我的臉，說道，「講大聲點！」

　　「先生，皮普。」

　　「你住在哪裡？指給我看！」他又問。

　　我指著遠處的村莊。

P.17

　　那個男人看了我一會兒，然後把我抓起來倒吊，掏空我的口袋。我的口袋裡什麼都沒有，只剩一小塊麵包。然後他把我擱在墓碑上，撿起麵包，狼吞虎嚥地啃了起來。我看著他，害怕得直打哆嗦，強忍著不哭。

　　「你媽呢？」

　　「先生，在那裡！」

　　他開始拔腿就跑，但又停了下來，回頭張望。

　　「先生，那裡！」我指著墳墓解釋道：「喬治安娜，那是我媽媽。」

　　「噢！你爸爸也在那裡嗎？」他一邊說，一邊走回來。

　　「先生，是的。」我回答。

　　「那你跟誰住？」他又問。

　　「和我姊姊喬·葛吉利太太，她是鐵匠喬·葛吉利的太太。」

　　「鐵匠，是吧？」他往下看著自己腳上的鐵環，說道。

　　接著，他抓起我的手臂，把我往後推。

　　「你知道什麼是銼刀吧？」

「先生，知道。」
「那你知道哪些是吃的吧？」
「先生，知道。」

P.18

「很好，幫我弄把銼刀跟一些吃的來。」他把我的手抓得更緊，說道：「明天一大早，把那些東西帶來給我。還有，不要跟別人說你碰到我。你要是不乖乖照我說的去做，我就把你的心臟挖出來，烤來吃！現在你說怎麼辦？」

他把我抓得很痛，所以我很快就答應他的要求，他這才放我走。我坐下來，望著他一瘸一拐地走到墓園的矮牆邊，翻過牆去。當他一消失在黑暗中，我立刻從墓碑上跳下來，一路狂奔，到家才停下來。

男人

- 你認為這個男人是誰？
- 他在墓園做什麼？
- 他為什麼要銼刀？
- 皮普會跟別人透露這件事嗎？

當我從墓園回來時，喬的鐵鋪已經關了。我打開廚房的門，走進去。喬正獨自坐在那裡。

P.19

「皮普，我太太正在找你呢。她已經出去好幾趟了。」他說。

「是嗎？」

「是啊，她這一次還帶上棍子！」他說。

就在那時候，門被推開，喬太太衝了進來，怒氣沖沖的。

P. 20

「你到底去哪裡了，你這個小畜牲？」
她大吼著。

「我只是去墓園。」我回答。

「墓園！」她重複了我的話，「這麼
晚了，這時間你在那裡做什麼？我花了
一個小時，到處找你！又要擔心，又要
工作！我照顧你，這就是我所得到的回
報！」

她把棍子放回角落，開始泡茶。她切
了兩塊麵包，塗上奶油。一塊給喬，一
塊給我。我想到墓園裡那個可怕的人，
嚇得不敢吃下手上的麵包。我知道自己
得把麵包留下來給他，所以我趁喬沒有
看到時，很快把麵包放進褲子的口袋裡。

隔天是聖誕節。我在天亮前就起床，
躡手躡腳地下樓。我偷拿了一些麵包、
一些起士和一塊豐美的豬肉派。豬肉派
是潘波趣叔叔送的，他是住在鎮上的富
商。接著，我到鐵鋪去拿銼刀。

那天早上很冷，霧比往常還濃。當我
到墓園時，我看到那個人就坐在前面的
墓碑上。他好像睡著了。於是我靜悄悄
地走向前，碰碰他的肩膀。他立刻跳起
來。結果，我看到的是不同的人！他的
穿著跟昨天那個人一樣，腳上也有個大
鐵環，但是年輕些。他一看到我，急忙
跑走，消失在霧裡。

P. 21

我朝墓園更裡面走去，沒多久，我就
看到那個人。我沒吭聲，把銼刀和一袋
食物遞給他。他把麵包和起士一起塞進
嘴裡，然後開始吃派。

「還好你吃得高興。」我說。

「是沒錯，孩子。謝謝你。」他回答，
嘴裡塞滿了派。

「我現在得走了。」我說，但他並沒有
在聽。

他急忙著把派吃完。我邁開步子離
去。我回頭看他時，他正用銼刀要把鐵
環從腳上撬開。

2. 逮捕

P. 22

　　那天早上稍晚，我和喬去上教堂，而喬太太忙著準備聖誕大餐。她都會在聖誕節那天邀請潘波趣叔叔和一些鄰居來家裡吃飯，所以有很多事要忙著張羅。

　　到了一點半的時候，我們所有人都坐到了餐桌前。桌上滿滿的美食，但少了一個派，我好怕東窗事發，根本無心享用。終於，我擔心的時刻到來了。

　　「潘波趣叔叔送了一個豐美的豬肉派給我們。」喬太太帶著一個大大的微笑，說道：「大家想來一點嗎？」

　　「好啊，當然！」聲音此起彼落響起。於是，她走進廚房去拿派。

　　我再也待不下去，我要趕快逃跑。我跑到門邊時，卻被堵住了。門外，有一位警佐和幾名士兵。他們帶著槍，警佐還拿著一副手銬。

P. 24

　　「鐵匠在哪裡？」他問道。

　　屋內的所有人都站了起來，跟著喬走到門邊，大夥感到很好奇。

　　警佐問喬：「鐵匠，你可以修好這些手銬嗎？這個鎖被弄壞了。沼澤附近有兩名囚犯，他們昨晚從囚船上逃走。我們得在天黑前逮捕他們，所以我們需要手銬。」

　　喬套上皮圍裙，立刻動手修理。他很快就修好了。

　　他把手銬遞給警佐，說道：「修好了。我可以跟你們一起去，幫忙尋找逃犯。」他又補了一句：「皮普，你也一起來。」

　　我們穿上外套，跟著警佐和士兵，來到了墓園。這時下著雪，天氣很冷。我們一到達時，就聽到遠處傳來說話聲，講得氣呼呼的。

　　士兵們立刻備好槍，跑了過去。當我們愈逼近，聲音就愈大，而且很清楚地聽得出來那裡只有兩個人。我當然知道他們是誰。

　　「他們在這裡，就在這裡！」一名士兵大喊道。

P. 25

　　那兩個人在滿是泥濘的水溝裡打架，似乎沒有注意到我們。士兵們跳進去，把他們拉開，然後銬上手銬。

雖然這兩個人滿身泥巴和血，但我還是馬上就認出來了。那個年輕人臉上青一塊紫一塊的，看起來全身無力，還得士兵幫忙才站得起來。

「他要殺我！」他說道，看著那個跟我說過話的囚犯。

「他亂說！是我抓到他的。我要他回囚船。他是流氓！」另一個囚犯回說。

那個年輕人好像很怕他的同伴。他微弱地不斷重複著說道：「他想殺我！」

「夠了！點上火把，我們得帶他們回囚船。來吧，快行動！」警佐說。

大約走了一個小時後，我們來到一棟小木屋，裡頭有個警衛，還有三、四名士兵。警佐在一個本子上做了些記錄後，警衛就把年輕人帶進囚船裡。當我們還在小屋裡等著時，那個跟我說過話的囚犯坐就在火堆前，他看著自己的腳，若有所思，一眼都沒瞧我。

P. 26

突然，他轉向警佐，開口說道：「我有話要說。我可以說話嗎？」

「你想說什麼，就說吧。」警佐回答。

「我從那邊村子的一個房子裡拿了一些食物，就是教堂旁邊的那間房子，鐵匠的家。」

喬驚訝地看著我。

囚犯說：「我很餓，所以拿了一個豬肉派和一些麵包。」接著，他又加了一句：「我覺得很抱歉。那個派很不錯。」

「很高興你喜歡。每個人都要吃東西的。」喬寬厚地回答他。

接著，警衛來帶走了他。我們站在窗戶旁看著。他爬上囚船，然後沒入其中。

監獄

▪ 這些著名的監獄在哪裡？從下列的國家中選選看：

____ a 阿爾卡特拉斯

____ b 伊芙堡

____ c 惡魔島

____ d 亞瑟港

____ e 魯賓島

1 法國

2 法屬圭亞那

3 南非

4 塔斯馬尼亞

5 美國

3. 造訪薩蒂斯莊園

P.27

一、兩年後的一個晚上，喬太太從鎮上的市場帶了一些有趣的消息回來，她說郝維申小姐要我去她家玩。喬和我驚訝地對望了一下。郝維申小姐是住在市郊一棟大屋裡的富家女，雖然每個人都聽過她的名字，卻鮮少有人知道她的長相。她是大門不出的。

「她怎麼認識皮普？」喬問。

「是潘波趣叔叔跟她提的，」喬太太回答道：「他前幾天去薩蒂斯莊園，郝維申小姐跟他說她想找個男孩到她家玩。他馬上就推薦皮普了。」

她一邊說，一邊在盆裡倒水。

「如果這孩子今天晚上還毫無感激之意，那他這輩子都不會懂得感激了！皮普，過來。」

她抓著我的肩膀，把我的頭壓進水裡。

「潘波趣叔叔就在外頭的馬車裡等你。」她一邊說，一邊用力地搓洗我的臉。

P.28

不一會兒，我就從頭到腳被洗得乾乾淨淨，還穿上了我最好的衣服。在向喬道別後，我爬上了馬車，坐在潘波趣叔叔的旁邊，然後出發往鎮上去。

隔天十點時，我就已經在薩蒂斯莊園的門外了。在我按了門鈴後，一個年輕的女孩出現。她長得很漂亮，我頓時害羞了起來。

「你是皮普？」她說。

從她跟我說話的方式，我發現她不只長得漂亮，而且很高傲。

她讓我進門，我靜靜地跟著她穿過庭院，進到屋內。我們走過好多道幽暗的長廊，然後爬了幾階樓梯。最後，我們來到一扇門邊。

「進去前，先敲門！」女孩說完，便離開。

我發現自己身處一個點著很多蠟燭的大房間裡。房裡所有的鐘都停在八點四十分，但實際上時間早已過了十點。

郝維申小姐就坐在一張小茶几旁的扶手椅上，她穿著一件材質奢華的嫁衣，頭上披著頭紗，白髮上別著褪色的花朵，只是這位新娘已非青春年華，她的嫁衣和頭紗不再白淨，而是因歲月而泛黃。她髮間的花朵，不再新鮮欲滴，顏色也失去了光澤。

P. 30

「是誰？」她問道。

「夫人，我是皮普。」

「走近一點！讓我看看你。」

我站在她面前，她盯著我看。然後她把手放在自己的左胸。

「你知道我摸的是什麼地方嗎？」她問道。

「夫人，是您的心。」

「已經破碎了！」她説。

接著，是好一陣子的沉默。最後，她説：「叫艾絲黛拉來。」

直呼那個女孩的名字，讓我覺得很難為情。她遲遲沒有回應，不過最後還是出現了。

「親愛的，過來這裡。跟這個孩子一起玩牌吧。」郝維申小姐説。

艾絲黛拉看起來很吃驚，「他不過是個鄉下孩子！看看他那雙粗糙的手。」

我覺得自己好像聽到了郝維申小姐低聲地跟她説，「那又怎樣？你可以讓他傷心。」但我不確定她是不是真的這樣説。

我們坐下來，開始玩牌。艾絲黛拉讓我覺得自己又蠢又笨拙，所以我一再出錯。很自然地，她贏了那場牌局。下一場，她又贏了。第三場也是。所以當郝維申小姐説我可以回家時，我很高興。

「下星期再過來吧。艾絲黛拉，在他離開前，給他弄點東西吃。」她説。

P. 32

艾絲黛拉要我在院子裡等她。幾分鐘後，她帶著一些麵包和肉回來。她把食物放在我前面的地上，我覺得自己像

隻受辱的狗，於是哭了出來。她不發一語，離開時，臉上帶著一抹勝利的神情。

當晚，我躺在床上想著白天在薩蒂斯莊園的一切。對我來說，那是個全新的世界。郝維申小姐和艾絲黛拉，她們和村子裡的人完全不一樣。她們沒有粗糙的雙手，也不窩在廚房裡吃東西。我開始為喬、姊姊和自己的出身感到羞愧。我想要成為薩蒂斯莊園那個世界裡的一分子。

4. 決鬥

P.33

接下來的那個星期三，我又來到了薩蒂斯莊園。那一天，樓下的一個房裡來了幾個人。從他們的言談中，我猜他們應該是郝維申小姐的親戚。

艾絲黛拉帶我上樓到郝維申小姐的房間，這時她突然問我：「喂！你覺得我怎麼樣？」

「我覺得你很漂亮，還有一點點刻薄。」我答道。

之後，她突然甩了我一耳光，又問：「你現在覺得我怎麼樣？」

「恕我不答，小姐。」

她轉身離開，留我一個人在郝維申小姐的房門外。

我走進房間，郝維申小姐一如往常地坐在小茶几旁。

她開口說道：「喔，皮普，日子過得真快。你準備好要玩牌了嗎？」

P.34

「女士，我想還沒有準備好。」我回答。

「那你如果不想玩，你就得做事。」她說：「到對面的房裡等我。」

就像屋子裡所有的房間一樣，那個房間也只用蠟燭照明。我看到一張長桌上鋪著白巾，中間擺著一個結婚蛋糕，但大大的蜘蛛網已經結滿了整個蛋糕。

郝維申小姐靜悄悄地走進來，把手搭在我肩上。我們緩慢地繞著桌子走了幾分鐘，然後她開口說：「皮普，你看到樓下那些人了嗎？他們是我的親戚帕啟士

137

家族。他們一年來看我一次，只希望在我死了後，能把錢留給他們。」

我不知道該說什麼。還好，艾絲黛拉正好出現。我們回到郝維申小姐的房裡玩牌。

我決定那天回家前要好好地看一下花園。出乎意外地，我竟在那裡碰到了一個男孩，跟我差不多年紀。他臉色蒼白，一頭金髮。

「來決鬥吧！」那個面色蒼白的年輕紳士看到我，就這麼說。

P.36

我不知所措。因為他看起來不太壯，我很怕自己會傷到他。但是他看起來好像非打不可，所以我揍了他。他摔到地上，鼻子開始流血。

不一會兒，他又重新站起來，準備繼續打。我又揍了他，而且加重力道。在他認輸放棄前，我大概又揍了他三、四次。

「你贏了。」他說。

「你還好嗎？」我問他：「要我幫你嗎？」

「謝謝你，不用了。」他回答道：「午安！」

在那之後，我還是繼續定期造訪薩蒂斯莊園，艾絲黛拉一直在那裡。她有時候對我還算客氣，但大多數的時候都很冷淡。她的情緒說變就變，我常常不知道該怎麼回應她，而郝維申小姐似乎非常樂於見到我這樣的窘態。

艾絲黛拉

- 艾絲黛拉和郝維申小姐之間是什麼關係？
- 艾絲黛拉為什麼對皮普那麼不友善？
- 郝維申小姐為什麼要艾絲黛拉和皮普當朋友？

P.37

喬太太和潘波趣叔叔認為，郝維申小姐對我的未來已有規畫。他們總是討論著她可能會為我做哪些事，這讓我很生氣，但背地裡我卻偷偷希望他們說對了。

之後有一天，郝維申小姐跟我說了：「皮普，你長高了，也該是開始工作的時候了。」

她知道喬希望我到鐵鋪和他一起做事，去當他的學徒。

「找葛吉利先生來這裡，帶上你的學徒合約，我想看看合約。」

「夫人，我該叫他什麼時候來？」

「我對時間沒概念，叫他盡快來就是了，你也可以一起來。」她說。

兩天後，喬和我一起回到了莊園。在郝維申小姐的屋裡，喬顯得格格不入，我為他感到尷尬又丟臉。當郝維申小姐問到他對我的規畫時，他竟不是對著郝維申小姐解釋，而是對著我講。我看到站在郝維申小姐身後的艾絲黛拉嘴角揚起，一絲殘酷的微笑讓我想逃離那個地方。

最後，有關我學徒工作的所有文件終於簽訂了，而我們也得以離開。

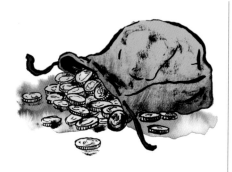

P. 38

郝維申小姐給了我一個小袋子，説道：「皮普，把這個給拿你的師傅，裡面有二十個基尼（舊英國金幣），這些都是你掙來的。再見了，皮普。」

艾絲黛拉帶我們到大門口，讓我們出去，然後她什麼都沒説地就轉身進去了。

當我們給喬太太看那些基尼時，她非常開心。從那天起，我就成了喬的學徒。她堅持當晚一定要在城裡的藍豬小館用餐。她還邀請了潘波趣叔叔和我們一起。這天晚上，每個人都很開心，只有我例外。雖然喬是全世界最好、最和善的人，但我仍強烈地感到他的那分工作一點都不適合我。

5. 遠大前程

P. 39

星期天時，喬和我常在到沼澤邊散步。那裡很舒服，也很安靜。當我看著水上的船隻時，總是想起造訪薩蒂斯莊園的那段時間。我忘不了艾絲黛拉。

一個星期日，我對喬説：「喬，我想我應該去探望一下郝維申小姐。我想謝謝她幫助了我。我明天可以休半天假嗎？」

我們其實不忙，所以他也就答應了。

隔天下午，我就過去了。莎拉·帕啟士小姐幫我開了門，帶我上樓，來到郝維申小姐的房間裡。那裡的一切和過去一模一樣。

「我希望你不是來跟我要東西的，」郝維申小姐説：「因為你什麼也拿不到。」

「我只是來告訴你，我在鐵鋪做得很順利。我很感激您。」我回答。

「嗯，你可以不時過來看看我。在你生日那天過來吧。」

P. 41

她看到我在張望房內四周。

「艾絲黛拉不在這了，她出國了。」她説：「她在學習如何當個淑女。皮普，她比之前更漂亮了喔。你想她嗎？」

她笑了起來。她喜歡看到我飽受煎熬的樣子。

之後，在我走路回家的一路上，我對自己的出身、工作還有一切，比以往更加感到不堪。

時間就這樣流逝了，我繼續在鐵鋪跟喬一起工作。每年生日那一天，我會去探望郝維申小姐。我希望能見到艾絲黛

拉，卻總是失望而歸。

有一天晚上，喬太太受到了襲擊。從那之後，她就沒法走路，也無法說話。所以一個村裡的女孩畢蒂，就來家裡照顧我們的起居。她是個性很好的女孩，也很聰明。

後來發生了一件事情，改變了我一生。

那是一個星期六的傍晚，喬和我正在藍豬小館裡，一個又高又黑的男人走了進來。他穿得很體面，像是城裡來的。

「這裡有叫皮普的人嗎？」他問館子的老闆。

「我就是皮普。」我說。

他轉過身來，仔細打量我後，說道：「我想私下跟你談談。我有件重要的事要告訴你，我們可以去你家嗎？」

P.42

我們沉默地走回家。喬打開了起居室的門，我們圍坐在桌旁。

「我叫傑格斯，是倫敦來的律師。皮普，我有個客戶非常關心你的前途。我得說，你有大好的前程！」

喬和我驚愕地看著彼此。他到底在說什麼？

「我的客戶，也就是你的贊助者，希望你能像紳士一樣受教育。」他繼續說：「因此，未來你將接收到一大筆錢。」

我的心開始撲通撲通地狂跳。「一定是郝維申小姐！」我猜。

「但是，有一些條件，」那個律師繼續說道：「首先，你要馬上離開村莊，到倫敦去。你永遠別想要查出你的贊助者是誰，還有，你要一直維持皮普這個名字。你接受這些條件嗎？」

「好吧。」我勉強說出。

「太好了！你需要一個私人教師、一個在倫敦的住所。我認識一個人，他可以幫你。他叫帕啟士，馬修·帕啟士。」傑格斯先生說。

P.43

那天晚上，喬告訴畢蒂我所得到的好運。他們兩人都很為我開心，但我知道喬其實也有點難過，他並不想失去我。我很慶幸還好有畢蒂在這陪著他和喬太太。

我在鎮裡度過最後的幾天，因為我打算做幾件新衣服。當一切都準備好時，我穿上新衣，去見郝維申小姐。

一如往常，當我按完門鈴後，還是由莎拉·帕啟士小姐為我開的門。她看到我時，很驚訝。

「我是來向郝維申小姐道別的，我要出遠門了。」我向她說明來意。

我走上她在樓上的房間，看到她和以往一樣坐在桌旁。

「皮普，你看起來很稱頭。」她看到我時，說道。

「我要去倫敦了，上次見到你之後，我的好運就來了。」我跟她說。

「你被有錢人收養了？」

「是的，我很感恩。」我回答。

「傑格斯先生是你的監護人嗎？」

「是的，郝維申小姐。」

「很好，大好的前程就在你前面了。好好表現，照著傑格斯先生的要求去做。再見了，皮普！你知道自己永遠都叫皮普吧。」她說。

P. 44

隔天一早，畢蒂五點就叫我起床。很快吃過早餐後，我就該離開了。在我上路時，喬和畢蒂就站在鐵鋪外，向我揮手。那一剎那，我突然覺得很感傷，差點就轉身走回去。

我大約在中午時分抵達倫敦。傑格斯先生的事務所就在驛馬站不遠的小不列顛，所以我決定步行到那裡。我對這座城市的第一印象並不好，街道狹小，髒亂而擁擠。空氣也很差，所有的一切都覆上一層灰。

一個辦事員跟我說傑格斯先生還在開庭。

「他很快就回來了，請在這裡稍後。」他說。

傑格斯先生的事務所不是個很舒適的

地方，所以我決定到外面走一走，看一看。

當我沿著一條小街閒逛時，經過了法庭所在的新門監獄，有一小群群眾就站在外面。我聽到傑格斯先生的名字不下一次地被提到。監獄外牆的後方，可以見到聖保羅大教堂的巨大黑色圓頂。

就在我準備回事務所之際，我看到我的監護人穿過對街，向我走來。

P. 46

「噢，皮普！你得和年輕的帕啟士先生先住在伯納德客棧幾天，星期一他就會帶你到他父親的寓所。我現在得回去開庭了，我的事務員威米克會招呼你。」他說。

伯納德客棧是一棟破舊的建築。威米克帶我到頂樓，就把我丟在帕啟士先生的房門外。門上貼了一張字條寫著「速回」，那表示我得等了。半個小時後，我聽到樓梯間有腳步聲，一個年輕人出現了。他看起來跟我差不多年紀，還拿著一些草莓。

「很抱歉，我遲到了。」他微笑著說：「我去柯芬園市場幫你買了些水果。在這裡！你可以幫我拿一下嗎？我來開門。」

6. 在倫敦的生活

P. 47

那個年輕人又拉又推，最後總算把門打開了。

他說：「請進。很抱歉，裡面沒有什麼家具，但還是希望你能舒服地待到星期一。我的收入微薄，而我父親也沒有太多錢給我。不管怎麼樣，這裡就是起居室，我們的臥室在那裡。噢，真不好意思！你還拿著那些草莓。讓我來吧。」

當我把水果遞給他時，我們才正視了對方。

「天啊！你是那個薩蒂斯莊園男孩！」他說。

「你是那個面色蒼白的年輕紳士。」

我們兩大笑起來。

「哇，太令人驚訝了！」他親切地握著我的手說。

P. 49

我馬上就喜歡上赫伯特·帕啟士了（赫伯特是這位年輕士紳的名字），他是個隨和、爽朗而開明的人。

那天傍晚，吃過晚餐後，我請他告訴我郝維申小姐的事。

「郝維申小姐的母親，在她襁褓時就過世了。在那之後，她父親盡全力滿足她，給了她所要的一切。郝維申先生富有又自傲，他的女兒也是。」他說。

「她是獨生女嗎？」我問。

「不，不是。他父親又再娶了，卻是在未曝光的情況下。在我印象中，那位女士是個廚娘，總之，他們生了個兒子。幾年後，第二任妻子也過世了。郝維申老爺決定將這個祕密婚姻和她有個同父異母的弟弟的事，告訴女兒。那個男孩從此成為家族的一分子。然而，他卻不學好，最後被父親逐出家門。」

「因此，在郝維申老爺過世時，他把大部分的財產留給了女兒。她同父異母的弟弟，為此對她非常不諒解。」

「後來又發生了什麼事？」

P. 50

「在那不久後，有位男士開始對郝維申小姐展開熱烈追求。他死纏爛打，不斷地說自己有多麼愛她。而她竟然相信了，還很快地深深愛上對方。當他向她求婚時，她答應了。我父親從來就不相信這位男士，因為他常向郝維申小姐要錢，而且都是一大筆錢。他說，那不是一位真正紳士該有的行為。但是，當我父親提醒她要注意時，她非常生氣。她把他趕出門，還不准他回去。就這樣，婚禮日期決定了，婚紗也買了，婚禮的邀請函也都發送出去了。大日子終於到了，但新郎卻沒到。他只留了一封信給她……」

我接著說：「……就在她打扮好迎接婚禮時，她收到了那封信。」

「就在八點四十分，之後，她將屋裡所有的鐘都停在那一刻。」赫伯特說。

「從此，她再也沒離開過那棟房子，這就是全部的經過？」我說。

「這就是我所知道的一切了。」赫伯特回答道。

P. 51

郝維申小姐

• 新郎在他給郝維申小姐的信中說了什麼？
• 這件事如何改變了郝維申小姐的一生？
• 你認為在這次事件後，她對男人的看法如何？

「那個男的現在還活著嗎？」

「我不知道。」

「那艾絲黛拉呢？」

赫伯特聳聳肩，「我只知道郝維申小姐收養了她。我的朋友，現在你對郝維申小姐了解的程度，就跟我一樣了。」

星期一一早，赫伯特帶我到他父親位於漢默史密斯的宅第。馬修·帕啟士先生頂著一頭凌亂的白髮，卻有著一張娃娃臉。不過，他的臉上帶著憂慮的神情。

「很高興見到你。」他微笑著說。他的微笑，讓我想到赫伯特。「請隨我來，你的房間在樓上。希望你會喜歡。」

我的確是喜歡，房間很舒適，還可以看到花園。帕啟士先生隨後向我介紹了別的房客，兩位名叫朱穆爾和史達塔的年輕人。他們兩人的房間和我同一樓層，他們也接受帕啟士先生的指導。

P. 52

在接下來幾天，我們更加了解彼此。朱穆爾出身於英格蘭西南部的富有人家，他高大、自負，動作遲緩又懶散。而史達塔卻完全相反，自然而然地，我喜歡和史達塔作伴，勝於和朱穆爾在一起。

兩、三天後，我和帕啟士先生進行了一段長談。他給了我不少好的忠告，包括倫敦值得造訪的地方，以及購物的好去處。他很和氣，又有耐性，我相信自己一定可以從他身上學到很多。

儘管我在漢默史密斯的房間待得很愜意，但我還是決定問問傑格斯先生，看我可不可以留下伯納德客棧的房間。我和赫伯特現在已經成了好朋友，我很喜歡和他待在一起。

「你需要買些家具。你需要多少錢？五鎊？十鎊？還是二十鎊？」我的監護人說。

「二十鎊已經綽綽有餘了。」我回答。

「威米克，給皮普先生二十鎊！」傑格斯先生打開辦公室的門，對外喊著。

那個事務員坐在自己的辦公桌前，吃著硬餅乾。他把那些餅乾塞進嘴裡，像塞郵件到信箱裡那般。雖然傑格斯先生

144

在場時，他的話很少，不過他是個很親切溫暖的人。

P. 54

那天，他主動地帶我參觀，當我們看到傑格斯先生事務所裡一些殺人犯的石膏頭像時，我們聊起了他的老闆。

「他邀你共進晚餐了嗎？」威米克問。

「還沒。」

「喔，那他很快就會向你提出邀請了，他也會邀請你那三位朋友。」他說：「到時候，餐點的樣式或許不多，但是他提供的食物，絕對都是最佳品質。這是可以確定的。還有，當你到那裡時，仔細地觀察一下他的管家。」

「為什麼？」我很好奇地問道：「可以看到什麼奇特的事嗎？」

「一頭被馴服的野獸。」

沒多久，我對傑格斯先生的管家的好奇心就被滿足了。當我再次拜訪我的監護人時，他提出共進晚餐的邀請。

他說：「到這裡碰面。」之後他又補上一句：「還有，帶你的朋友們。」

傑格斯先生的住家在蘇活區。他住在附三間暗房的一樓屋子裡。當我們抵達時，在最好的那間房裡，餐桌已經擺設成晚宴的樣子了。

P. 55

我們入座後，管家送上第一道菜。我很仔細地觀察她，她差不多四十歲左右，有著凌亂的長髮，讓我聯想到了莎翁劇作《馬克白》中的女巫。

用完餐後，當她在收拾餐盤時，傑格斯先生突然抓住她的手。

「莫莉，讓他們看看你的手腕。」他說。

「請不要這樣，大人！」她低聲地說。

他又下了一次命令。莫莉把自己的手翻過來讓我們看。其中一隻手腕上，有一些深深的傷疤。

「各位，這是堅強的手腕。」傑格斯先生說：「這雙手，也有著強大的力量。在我這一生中所看過的許多手當中，不管是男人或女性，我沒看過比這個更堅韌的。謝謝你，莫莉。你現在可以離開了。」

九點半整，傑格斯先生送我們回家。大約一個半月後，朱穆爾結束了帕啟士先生的修業，返回家鄉。對於他的離開，我一點都不難過。我想史達塔也是。

145

7. 改變

P. 56

一個星期一早上，我收到了一封信。是畢蒂寫來的，上頭寫著：

親愛的皮普先生：

葛吉利先生要我寫信告訴您，他將前往倫敦與您相會。他將於星期二上午九點，抵達伯納德客棧。您可憐姐姐的狀況，與您離開時相差不遠。我們每晚都談到您，想著您在做什麼、說些什麼。親愛的皮普先生，全部就是這樣。

畢蒂敬上

P. 57

我很慚愧地說，我不是很高興收到這個消息。我不想見到喬。我不想讓他打擾我的新生活，他不屬於這一切。但是，已經來不及寫信阻止他來了。

當天傍晚，我從漢默史密斯進到倫敦市區，做好等他來的準備。隔天早上，我將起居室打點成最好的狀態，並確定早餐已經擺放在桌上。就在九點前，我聽到喬走上樓梯的聲音。他站在門外好久，最後才敲門。我上前迎他入內。

「喬！你好嗎，喬？」

「皮普！你好嗎，皮普？」他答道。

當他用力地握著我的手時，他那善良真誠的臉龐，看起來是那麼的開心。

「喬，我好高興能見到你。鐵鋪一切都好嗎？」

當他訴說喬太太和畢蒂的近況，一抹畏懼的神情突然出現在他臉上。我轉身看到赫伯特站在房門口。我對寒酸的喬沒來由地生起氣來。

我將他介紹給我的朋友認識，然後一起就座共進早餐。顯然地，喬跟我們在一起時非常不自在。他不知該說什麼好，還不時地將食物掉在地上。他的侷促不安，只讓我更覺得尷尬，但我卻袖手旁觀。

P. 59

我也知道自己這樣做是很殘酷的，所

以當赫伯特離席，再度剩下我們兩人獨處時，我開心多了。接著，他說起了這次來訪的原因。

「我見到郝維申小姐了，皮普。艾絲黛拉小姐已經回來了，她想見你。」

當喬講完話時，我感覺自己的臉都紅了。

「皮普，這就是我來這要說的話。現在我該回去了。」他一邊說，一邊站起身來，戴上帽子。

「你不留下來吃晚飯嗎？」我問道。

「不了，皮普，我在這格格不入。」他說：「這身衣服也不適合我，鐵鋪、灶間、沼澤，才是我該待的地方。再見了，皮普。」

之後他和藹地摸摸我的臉頰，就離開了。

格格不入

- 找個夥伴討論，想想一些讓你覺得格格不入的狀況，說明為什麼會這樣。
- 談談你自己感到格格不入的經驗。

P. 60

隔天，我早早就起床，買了驛馬車的票。整趟旅途中，我思索著落腳處。「我應該回鐵鋪。」我本想著，但隨後我開始編出許多自己應該待在鎮上的理由。因此，當我一抵達，我就直接前往藍豬小館了。

翌日早晨，我步行到薩蒂斯莊園。郝維申小姐已經在等我了，還有一位優雅的女士坐在她身旁。由於她低著頭，我看不到她的臉。

「進來吧，皮普！」郝維申小姐說：「你過得好嗎？」

「郝維申小姐，我聽說您想見我，所以我立刻就來了。」

「喔？」她說著，眼神卻飄移到身旁的女士上。

那位女士跟著抬頭一望。之後我看到了，原來是艾絲黛拉，但卻非我昔日所認識的那個艾絲黛拉！她不再是一個氣焰高張的年輕女孩，而是一個美麗的淑女了。她將手遞過來，我親吻了一下。剎那間，我覺得自己又變回了那個笨拙的鄉下孩子。

「她變了嗎？」郝維申小姐問道。

我可以看出她很樂於見到我的窘態。我回答：「我剛進來時，還認不出她來。但是我現在看到了以前的……」

「什麼？」郝維申小姐說：「你該不會是要說以前那個艾絲黛拉吧？她既高傲又刻薄呢！」

P. 62

「那他也變了嗎？」她反問艾絲黛拉。

「變了很多。」那位年輕的女士看著我，微笑地說道。

「比較沒那麼粗俗了？」

艾絲黛拉笑了。

當我們坐下來聊天時，我發現要將過去與現在區隔開來，著實困難。再次見到她，讓我想起自己過去那個想變富有、過紳士生活的夢想——也就是這個夢想，使得我覺得喬和鐵鋪是丟臉的。我領悟到，原來艾絲黛拉是我的一部分——我人生的一部分。

郝維申小姐要我留下來吃晚餐。

「你可以晚上再回鎮上，然後明天搭車回倫敦。」她說。

讓我驚訝的是，她接著說：「傑格斯先生等等就到了，因為我們有些事要商量。你們兩可以有一個小時的時間到花園走走。」

當我們在棄置的花園沿著小徑散步時，艾絲黛拉說：「我記得見過你在這打架。這樣說可能有點奇怪，不過我還頗樂在其中的。」

「赫伯特和我現在已經是很好的朋友了。」

「是嗎？有人跟我說，你是他父親的門生。」

P. 63

當我走在她身旁時，還是可以感受到我們之間的差異。她對自己很有信心，也很清楚自己人生的定位，而我就像她的隨從。

「你還記得我來到這裡的第一天嗎？」我問她，「你把我弄哭了。」

「不，我不記得了。」她回答。

「你一定記得！」

「不，不記得。你應該知道，我是沒有心的人。這大概跟我的回憶有關。」她說。

「但是像你這麼美的人，一定有心的。」雖然我嘴上這麼說，但我知道這種話說出口還是很蠢。

「噢！我當然有心，可以被刺傷、被射穿，而且它要是停擺了，我的命也沒了。」艾絲黛拉說：「不過，你知道我指的是什麼。我不溫柔，沒有憐憫心，也沒有感情。」

她看著我，有那麼一刻，我想起了另一張面孔。我想那一定是郝維申小姐，但不，不是她那張臉。到底是誰，我也不知道。

我們又繞著花園多走了一會兒，然後進到屋子裡。

郝維申小姐在擺著長桌的房間裡。當艾絲黛拉回房為晚餐做準備時，我和她待在一起。

P. 65

「她美嗎？你愛慕她嗎？」她問我。

「很難不愛慕。」我回答。

之後她把我拉過去，滿懷激動地說：「愛她！愛她！如果她喜歡你，就愛她吧！如果她傷害你，還是要愛她！如果她讓你傷心欲絕，一樣要愛她！皮普，我收養她，就是為了讓她被人愛。」

她把我拉得更靠近他，低聲說道：「你知道什麼是愛嗎？愛，就是付出你全部

的心，就跟我以前一樣。」

之後她突然站起來，放聲大哭。這時，我聽到門關上的聲音，我轉頭看到我的監護人就站在房裡。郝維申小姐立刻坐下來，回復沉默，看起來有些尷尬。

「傑格斯，你還真準時！和皮普一起用餐吧。」她說。

在往廚房路上，傑格斯先生跟我說，郝維申小姐從不讓人看到她吃東西或喝東西的樣子。

「她會在夜裡四處遊走，找到什麼就吃什麼。」他說。

「我可以問你一個問題嗎，傑格斯先生？」

「可以，不過我可能不會回答。」

「艾絲黛拉姓郝維申嗎？」

「是。」

P. 66

晚餐後，在我跟傑格斯先生回藍豬小館前，艾絲黛拉和我又打了一會兒牌。那天夜裡，我躺在床上，一直想起郝維申小姐的話：「愛她！愛她！」

「我愛她！我愛她！」我對自己的枕頭不斷重複了上百次。「有一天，我要喚醒她沉睡的心。」我開心地這樣想著，「但那天又會是什麼時候呢？」

翌日，傑格斯先生和我搭上馬車，回到了倫敦。

皮普與艾絲黛拉

- 皮普和艾絲黛拉有任何共同點嗎？
- 他們在哪些方面有所不同？
- 皮普該如何喚起艾絲黛拉「沉睡的心」？

P. 67

在造訪薩蒂斯莊園後不久，我就收到一封信。我認不出信封上的筆跡，但我猜出來信者的身分。我打開信，讀道：

> 我將於明日抵達倫敦。我相信您已經答應郝維申小姐，你會到至驛馬站接我。郝維申小姐要我代為問候您。
>
> 艾絲黛拉敬筆

149

隔天，我在她的馬車抵達前幾小時，就到達了驛馬站。當我終於看到她下車時，我覺得她比以前更美了。

「我要去里奇蒙，你得雇輛馬車帶我去。」他告訴我，「郝維申小姐給了我這筆預算，錢在這裡！我們要遵守她的指示，皮普。你和我，都沒有決定的自由！」

我去找了輛馬車，然後就啟程。當我們路過漢默史密斯時，我指出帕啟士先生的宅第給她看。

P. 68

「那裡離里奇蒙很近。」我跟她說：「希望改天能再見到你。」

「喔，當然，你一定要來。整個家族都耳聞你的事了。」她說。

這段路程很短，時間過得太快。幾分鐘後，我們就抵達目的地了，艾絲黛拉的身影沒入於屋內。我站了好一會兒，望著房子，心裡琢磨著。雖然我想一輩子和她住在那屋子裡，但我也知道，只要和她在一起，我就會一直吃盡苦頭。

8. 祕密計畫

P. 69

我現在對於自己擁有大好前程的這種想法，已經非常習慣了，所以我盡情地揮霍。赫伯特也是。結果，我們兩人債台高築，背上了鉅額負債。我們的房裡到處都是帳單，有時候我們會一起坐下來把帳單整理好，這樣做讓我們覺得好過些。

一天傍晚，當我們正在欣賞面前那一疊疊整齊的帳單時，一封鑲著黑邊的郵件送到了。

「喔，天啊！這看起來應該是壞消息。」赫伯特說。

那封信通知了我姊姊過世的消息。她並未帶給我太多美好的回憶，但這個消息還是震撼了我，讓我感到悲傷。我立刻寫信給喬，告訴他，下星期一的喪禮我一定會到。

當我返家時，他獨自一個人坐在廚房的一角。

「親愛的喬，你還好嗎？」我說。

他拉著我的手，難過得說不出話來。

P. 71

姊姊葬在墓園中，就在我父母的旁邊。結束後，潘波趣叔叔和幾個鄰居回到鐵鋪吃點東西。當喬、畢蒂和我終於可以獨處時，喬脫掉他一直穿著的黑色大斗篷。我們坐在起居室，有好一會兒，都沒有人出聲。

後來，喬和我到鐵鋪去。我們聊著無關緊要的話題，他開始放鬆下來。當我問他，我晚上可不可以睡在自己的舊房

間時,他顯得很高興。

　　我隔天一早去向他道別時,他已經在鐵鋪工作了。我答應會盡快回來看他,也會常回來。

　　「皮普,永遠都不嫌快,也不嫌太常。」他説。

　　當我離開時,我想著自己的承諾。我真的打算遵守嗎?我自己都不以為然。

　　好幾個星期過去了,赫伯特和我繼續砸錢,也不打算處理我們的債務。

　　在我二十一歲生日的前一天,我收到了威米克的訊息。他要我隔天到傑格斯先生事務所一趟。我完全不知道會發生什麼事。

　　「皮普,今天我得改口稱你皮普先生

了。恭喜你,皮普先生!」傑格斯先生説。

P.72

　　我們握了手,我向他道謝。

　　「現在,我的年輕朋友,你有什麼想問我的嗎?」我的監護人開始説。

　　「你今天要告訴我,我的贊助人是誰了嗎?」

　　「不,問點別的。」

　　「那你會盡快告訴我嗎?」

　　「我無法回答。問點別的。」傑格斯先生説。

　　我環顧四周,手足無措地感到困窘。但看來我就是得問他問題。

151

「先生，那有什麼東西是要給我的嗎？」

「我就是在等你這句話！」他開心地說。他叫威米克拿帳簿過來。

「你的名字已經被威米克登記在這簿子上很多次了，我想你應該是負債累累了吧。我說對了嗎？」他說。

「先生，我想是吧。」

「拿著。」他一邊說，一邊遞給我一張紙，「現在看一下，告訴我這是什麼。」

「鈔票。」我回答：「五百鎊的鈔票。」

「這是你的生日禮物。」傑格斯先生說：「每年你都會收到同樣金額的錢。我將負責轉交給你，直到你的贊助人決定現身為止。再見了，皮普。」

P. 74

我在離去之前，停下來和威米克說話。我心裡有個想法，而我需要聽聽他的意見。

「威米克先生，我想問問你的看法。我想幫助一個朋友。」我說。

接著，我告訴他赫伯特的事。我解釋說我為他感到惋惜，他是個很好的人，也是個很貼心的朋友。

「我的朋友想做生意，但是他發現沒有錢就很難起頭。我現在有錢了，所以我想助他一臂之力。你覺得我可以怎麼做？」我繼續說。

威米克沉默了一下，之後說道：「皮普先生，你人真好。我認識一個人，他可能可以幫你。讓我先跟他談談。」

一個星期後，威米克傳來了訊息，要我過去找他。

「皮普先生，好消息！我的朋友認識一個名叫克拉瑞克的年輕商人，他剛創立了一間小公司，正在找合夥人投資。」他說。

聽起來剛好適合赫伯特。但我不想讓他知道我所做的一切，所以我私下去和威米克的朋友會面，祕密安排所有事宜。

P. 75

他告訴我說，他成為了克拉瑞克先生的合夥人，那一天，他那張快樂的臉，我永遠不會忘記。當天晚上，我躺在床上時，我哭了。我終於用錢做了件好事。

皮普的前程

- 和朋友討論以下的問題：
- 皮普的前程，如何改變了他的一生？
- 他的前程，又如何改變了他的為人處事？

在艾絲黛拉抵達倫敦後，我大部分的時間都待在里奇蒙。我並不是她唯一的愛慕者，追求她的人很多，不過只有我可以直呼她的名字。只不過，這並不表示她對我青睞有加。她對我的態度，仍然很差，因為她知道我深愛著她。儘管有她在時，我從未享受過片刻的快樂，但我卻從未停止想和她在一起的念頭。

一天晚上，我們一起去參加里奇蒙的一場舞會。我發現朱穆爾也在那裡，這讓我很吃驚。他的眼神整晚都不曾從艾絲黛拉身上移開過，而她似乎也很得意能得到他的注意。

P. 76

「艾絲黛拉，你為什麼要勾引那邊那個人？他不是個好人，沒有人喜歡他。」我説。

「我沒有勾引他！」她回答。

「你有，你對他笑的次數，比對我笑還多。」我説。

她轉過來生氣地看著我：「你要我騙你、耍你嗎？」

「你是在騙他、耍他嗎，艾絲黛拉？」

「沒錯，還有其他許多人。除了你以外，他們全部都是。但我不會再多説了。」

9. 不速之客

P. 77

在我二十三歲那一年的一個夜裡，我的人生轉了一個彎。

赫伯特和我現在一起住在河邊一棟房子的頂樓。那晚，我獨自在家，因為赫伯特去法國出差了。就在我聽著風吹拂過河水的聲音時，突然聽到樓梯上傳來腳步聲。

我拿起了燈，走出去看看是誰。

「有人在那嗎？」我喊著。

「有。」從下方的黑暗處傳來一個聲音。

「你要去哪一層樓？」

「去頂樓，皮普先生。」

我舉燈照著台階,照到一位男子的臉。我認不出是誰,但那人的表情看起來好像很高興見到我。

他衣服穿得很暖和,但不太體面。他一頭灰色的長髮,皮膚因長時間處在戶外而顯得黝黑。我猜他大概六十歲左右。

「你找我嗎?」我問他。

P. 79

「是的,我是來找你的,先生。」他回答。

我領著他走到屋裡。他看了看四周,對著看到的情景笑了笑。然後,做出奇怪的舉動,向我伸出雙手。

「你要做什麼?」我往後退了幾步。我覺得他可能瘋了。

他看起來很不解,用手撥了撥頭髮。「讓我喘口氣,再告訴你。」他回答說。

他在火爐旁的椅子上坐下來。剎那間,我認出他是誰了!他是墓園裡那個被判刑的囚犯。

他看出我表情有異,朝我走來,再次伸出他的手。這次,我握住了他的雙手。他親吻了我的手,繼續握著。

「你幫助過我,皮普,我不曾忘記過。」他說。

他看著我,眼神帶著濃厚的感情,但我對他並沒有感覺。我抽回雙手,說道:「你不需要特地來道謝,你要了解……」

「了解什麼,皮普?」

「我的人生已經不一樣了,我現在不能

和你做朋友了。你看起來又濕又累，你在離開之前，想要喝點什麼嗎？」

「謝謝。」他的眼神一直停留在我身上，緩慢地說出。

P. 80

我倒了兩杯酒，一杯給他，一杯給我自己。當我把杯子遞給他時，我訝異地看到他眼裡滿是淚水。

「如果我的話讓你受傷了，我很抱歉。我不是故意要如此失禮的。」我說。

當我將杯子舉到唇邊時，他伸出手。我握住他的手，之後他才喝了酒。

不速之客

- 皮普的訪客有何感受？
- 他對皮普抱有什麼樣的期待？

「你在做什麼工作？」我問他。

「我一直在澳洲，我在那邊牧羊。」他說。

「希望你做得不錯，是嗎？」

「我做得很好。」

「很高興聽到你這麼說。」

之後他笑著說：「我可以問一下，我們在沼澤見面之後，你是怎麼發展得這麼好的？」

「我有個贊助者。」我有點不好意思地說。

「我可以問是誰嗎？」

P. 81

我遲疑了一下後，回答說：「我不知道他的名字。」

囚犯仍笑著問：「我可以猜猜你的收入有多少嗎？第一位數字是五嗎？」

我的心臟開始跳得飛快。

「那你有監護人嗎？或許是位律師？他的名字是 J 開頭的嗎？」

P. 82

剎那間，我突然知道他為何而來了。我站了起來，扶著椅背。我說不出話，也無法呼吸，開始覺得天旋地轉。在我跌倒前，他抓住了我，把我扶到沙發上去。

「沒錯，皮普，就是我。」他貼近我的臉，說道：「是我讓你當上紳士，你從沒想過那個人就是我嗎？」

「沒有，不曾這樣想過。」我小聲地說。

「皮普，對我來說，你就像兒子一樣。」他繼續說道：「當我被遣送到世界的另一端時，我總是想著你。我辛苦工作了許多年。後來，我的主人讓我自由，還給了我一些錢。我開始為自己工作，做得很成功。」

他又再度握住我的手並親吻。當他碰我時，我只感到厭惡想吐。我無法將這男人是個罪犯的念頭拋開。

「我是為了你而工作的，皮普。」他繼續說：「想著你正花著我賺來的錢，這讓我很快樂。」他指著我手上的戒指，「黃金和鑽石！一個紳士該帶的戒子。看看這屋子。」

我微弱地笑著。他又繼續說著：「我下定決心，有一天一定要回來看看你。皮普，對我來說，要離開那些並不容易，而且也很不安全。但我已經下定決心，也終於付諸實現了。」

P. 83

我不知道該說什麼。我的腦子亂成一片。

他說：「是的，我成功了，但是我好累。我已經在船上待了好幾個月了。」

「我的朋友赫伯特現在不在家，你可以睡在他房裡。」我說。

「他明天不會回來，是吧？」

「對，明天不會回來。」

「因為我們一定要非常謹慎。」他把一隻長長的手指放在我的胸前，沉穩地說。

「為什麼？」我問。

「我曾因為企圖殺人而被判終生驅逐，如果被他們發現，我會被吊死。」他說。

這讓我感覺更加糟糕。我討厭這個人，而他冒著生命危險，卻只為了跟我在一起！

我帶他到赫伯特的房裡，給了他一些乾淨的衣服。五分鐘後，他睡著了。我走出去，坐在即將熄滅的火爐旁。我因為太痛苦而無法入眠。我試著思考，但是腦子裡只有一團亂。

一、兩個小時後，可怕的事實逐漸變得明朗。郝維申小姐對我或我的未來，毫不感興趣；她對我和艾絲黛拉，也沒有什麼計畫。她只是利用我們來為她報復男人！

P. 84

最後，我還是睡著了。當我醒來時，時鐘正指著五。我起身，看了看赫伯特的房裡，那位囚犯還在那裡。

「我無法藏匿他太久。」我思索著：「人們會猜測他的身分。」

房裡又冷又黑，於是我生了火，等他起床。

當他起床時，陽光透過窗戶，照進屋內。這男人又再度讓我感到厭惡了起來。

「我不知道你的名字，」我發問，試著不看他。

「我叫馬格維奇。阿貝爾·馬格維奇。」他回答。

「你打算在英國待多久？」

「多久？」他驚訝的重複道：「我不回去了，我要留下來。」

「你不能留在這裡。」我急忙說：「過幾天，我的朋友就回來了。我會幫你找住的地方。」

他看似開心地接受這個結果，所以我就出門去幫他找住所。接下來的五天，我們都待在屋裡，因為我不敢讓他出門。之後，赫伯特就回來了。

當我向赫伯特說明馬格維奇的事時，赫伯特臉上驚訝的表情真是筆墨難以形容。但是我可以從他的神情看出來，他和我一樣不喜歡馬格維奇。

我們一起共進晚餐，接著我便將客人帶到他的住處。當我回到家時，赫伯特張開雙臂等候著我。能擁有他這樣一位朋友，我真是幸運！

P. 85

朋友

- 你最好的朋友是誰？
- 你最喜歡他們哪一點？

「我該怎麼做？」我問赫伯特，「我不想再拿這個男人的錢了。但是如果他發

156

現這一點，可能會殺了我！他有暴戾性格。」

「答案很明顯，我的朋友，馬格維奇一定要離開英國。」赫伯特回答。

「他不會心甘情願離開的，他太喜歡我了。」我說。

「那你就得容忍他了。」赫伯特回答道。

隔天，馬格維奇跟我們述說了他這的一生。

「我不知道我是在哪裡出生的，也不知道是誰幫我取的名字。我不曾擁有過一個家。當我還是小男孩的時候，就要靠偷竊苟活。我被逮捕，入監服刑。之後，我不斷的進出監獄。有一天，我遇到一個叫作康佩森的男子。他的行為舉止和談吐看似紳士，但事實並非如此。當我告訴他，我想要找份工作，他問我願不願意當他的合夥人。猜他是做哪一行的？詐騙！他是箇中翹楚，他讓別人賣命工作，像我就是，然後自己拿走全部的錢。那個人是個狼心狗肺的人。我一直不斷的工作，一直處在危險之中。我的太太甚至……」

P. 86

他停頓了幾秒鐘，看起來很慌亂。

「但你們不需要知道她的事。反正，最後我們都被抓了。在審判的過程中，他把所有的責任都推給我。因為他穿得很體面，談吐也得宜，法官就相信了他。法官判了康佩森七年的刑期，卻給了我十四年的刑期。我告訴康佩森：『我會為此打爛你的臉。』我們被關在同一艘囚船上，但我沒見著他。某個晚上，我逃跑了，康佩森也逃跑了，但當時我並不知道。皮普，告訴我，你還記得嗎？隨後，我在沼澤找到他，打爛他的臉。這就是我被終生驅逐的原因。」

赫伯特在一本書的封面上寫了字，靜靜地把書推向我，我看到了：

康佩森，這是郝維申小姐的情人的名字。

157

10. 危險！

P. 87

我想在離開這個國家之前，和艾絲黛拉、郝維申小姐談一談。赫伯特了解我的想法，而且在我去薩蒂斯莊園時，他好心地主動要幫我照顧馬格維奇。

出乎我意料之外，當驛馬車抵達藍豬小館時，我第一個見到的人竟然是朱穆爾。我立刻猜出他出現在這裡的原因。我們不甚和氣地稍微交談了一會，然後他就離開了。

我沒有停下來吃點東西，就直接往薩蒂斯莊園走去。我想請郝維申小姐幫個忙，另外，我也有話要告訴艾絲黛拉。

郝維申小姐在她房內，而艾絲黛拉就坐在她身旁。她們看到我，很驚訝。

「皮普，什麼風把你吹來了？」郝維申小姐問道。

「郝維申小姐，你一直認為帕啟士家族只是覬覦你的錢，其實你錯了。我花了很多時間和他們相處，我可以說，馬修·帕啟士先生是我見過最善良誠實的人。他的兒子，赫伯特，也是我最好的朋友。」我開始說。

P. 89

郝維申小姐看起來不太自在。「你想要幫他們做什麼？」她問。

「如果你有一些多餘的錢，你可以做一些對赫伯特有幫助的好事。我在兩年前開始資助他，但是我已經無法再繼續幫他了。我不能告訴你原因。」我說。

郝維申小姐看了看火爐，然後瞧向我。「還有呢？」她問。

我轉向她說：「艾絲黛拉，我愛你。從第一天見到你時，我就已經愛上你了。我從未奢望能擁有你，但是我希望你能知道。」

艾絲黛拉說：「當你說你愛我，我聽得懂那些話，但是這種話並未觸動過我的心。我一點不在乎你的感受。我之前就跟你說過了。」

「艾絲黛拉，那你愛本特利·朱穆爾嗎？」

她看著郝維申小姐，沒有立刻回答我。隨後她說：「我要嫁給他了。」

「艾絲黛拉，親愛的艾絲黛拉！別讓郝維申小姐在這件事上影響了你。你值得比朱穆爾更好的男人。我無法忍受想像你和那個男人在一起的情景。」

「這是我做的決定，不是我養母。」她冷冷地說道：「反正你很快就會忘了我。」

「不會！」我激動地喊出：「你是我的一部分，艾絲黛拉。雖然你傷過我是事實，但我從沒想過要忘了你。」

P. 90

艾絲黛拉面無表情。然而，當我要離開房間時，我看到郝維申小姐臉上露出震驚的神情。

情感

- 和夥伴討論。當人們感受到以下的感覺時，他們會怎麼做？
  - 驚嚇？　　害怕？
  - 興奮？　　憤怒？
- 寫下來，和班上同學分享你的想法。

我決定要徒步走回倫敦，因為我想要和我的不快獨處。當我終於到家時，已經是半夜了。正當我要走過大門時，警衛攔住了我。

「先生，有人留了張紙條給你。」他一邊說，一邊將紙條遞給我。

我打開紙條，立刻認出是威米克的字，紙條上寫著：「不要回家！」

P.91

為什麼我不能回家？我有危險嗎？馬格維奇有危險嗎？我突然感到害怕。我快步地走回街上，打電話叫了一台哈克尼馬車，請駕駛帶我去位於科文特花園的旅社。

我整夜沒什麼睡，當天微亮時，我立刻去找威米克。他告訴我，有人盯上我的房子。我的心撲通撲通的跳著。我想一定是康佩森，他知道馬格維奇在這裡。他想要在馬格維奇找到他之前，先殺了他。我看得出來威米克知道我在想什麼。

他繼續說著：「我已經建議赫伯特把你的客人帶到一個比較安全的地方，我相信他已經把他帶到他未婚妻家去了。」

赫伯特的未婚妻名叫克萊拉，住在格林威治附近。我決定立刻趕到那裡。

赫伯特開了門，直接把我帶進起居室。

他說：「克萊拉和她父親在樓上。他生病了，下不了床。」

「那馬格維奇呢？他還好嗎？」我焦急地問著。

「他沒事。他見到你應該會很開心，來吧！」赫伯特回答道。

P.92

我跟著他上樓，往頂樓的小房間走去。馬格維奇坐在火爐邊，看起來冷靜自在。他很高興見到我。

我說：「馬格維奇，你相信傑格斯先生和威米克嗎？」

「喔，相信，他們什麼都知道了。」他回答。

「我今天早上見到威米克了，他跟我說了一些壞消息。馬格維奇，有人知道你在這裡。留在這裡，對你來說太危險

了。你要盡快離開這個國家。」我接著很快地補上一句，「我當然會陪你一起。」

P. 93

我預料他會拒絕離開，但是他也知道自己身處危險之中。

「皮普，我有個計畫。你和我都很會駕船，我們可以自己帶著馬格維奇順著河離開。我們都不想其他人知道他逃跑了，對吧？你要立刻弄一艘船來，如果你開始每天在河上來來回回，人們就會認得你。之後等我們要和馬格維奇一起離開時，他們就不會起疑了。」赫伯特說。

P. 94

我喜歡赫伯特的主意，馬格維奇也喜歡這個計畫。

「太好了！這就是我們接下來要做的事。」我說：「現在我得走了，馬格維奇。你和克萊拉、赫伯特一起待在這裡，這裡很安全。」

「親愛的孩子，」他牽起我的手說：「不知道我們何時才能再見，我不想跟你道別。所以，我只說晚安！」

「晚安！赫伯特會居中幫我們傳訊。」

他站在最上層的階梯上，目送我們離開。我當下的感受，連我自己都感到驚訝。離開他，竟讓我感到焦慮又憂傷，我居然不再對他充滿憎惡了。

「從他第一次出現在這裡開始，我改變了許多。」我一邊走回家，一邊這樣想著。

隔天，我弄到一艘船。我開始定期將船開到河上，有時候自己一個人，有時候和赫伯特一起。

一個晚上，在河上練習後，我遇見了傑格斯先生。他邀我共進晚餐。

「威米克也會一起來。」他說。

當我和傑格斯先生抵達時，他已經先到了。我們圍著桌子坐下，莫莉立刻就送上餐點。

當我們開始用餐時，傑格斯先生轉向威米克，說道：「郝維申小姐的短箋，你交給皮普了嗎？」

「還沒，還在我的口袋裡。」辦事員答道：「在這裡！」

P. 95

「只有兩行字，皮普。」傑格斯先生說：「郝維申小姐有事找你商討，生意上的事。她說你懂的。」

「我明天去一趟。」我希望這生意上的事和赫伯特有關。

莫莉走進來，將另一道餐點擺在桌上。她手部的動作，吸引了我的注意，讓我想起了另一雙也是以相同方式動作的手。我更仔細地觀察她。那雙眼睛！好熟悉的眼神。之後突然間，我想起來了，那是艾絲黛拉的眼神！

回家的路上，我要求威米克跟我說說莫莉的事。

他說：「大約二十年前，她企圖謀殺一個女人。傑格斯先生是她的律師，為她辯護，還打贏了官司。之後，她就開始為他工作。我相信她有個孩子。有些人說，她是為了要報復丈夫，才殺人的。」

「那孩子是男孩，還是女孩？」我問道。

「是個女孩。」

11. 河道之旅

P. 96

隔天，當我見到郝維申小姐時，她看起來不太一樣，不再那麼高傲，似乎還有些怕我。

「皮普，上次你在這裡的時候，你說我可以做些對你朋友有幫助的好事。是什麼？」

我向她解釋，赫伯特是如何成為克拉瑞克先生公司合夥人的那段祕史。

「我希望可以自己支付完所有的款項，但是最近我的處境變了，無法完成這個由我自己起頭的工作。」我說。

「所以呢？還需要多少錢？」她問。

我有點不敢告訴她金額，看起來是很大一筆數字。

「九百英鎊。」

她站起來，走向書桌。一、兩分鐘後，她走回來，手上拿著一張紙。

「把這個拿給傑格斯先生，他會把錢給你。」她說。

在我道謝之前，她繼續說：「皮普，我把名字寫在那張紙的下方。如果你可以在我的名字下面寫上『我原諒她』，就請這麼做吧。」

P. 97

「郝維申小姐！我現在就可以寫。」我說：「在我這一生中，也曾犯過錯，也需要被原諒。我怎麼會不原諒您呢？」

她握住我的手，將手拉近自己的臉。她哭了。

「喔！我到底做了什麼？」她啜泣地說。

我知道她心裡想到的，是我和艾絲黛拉。

當她心情稍微平復一些，我問她：「郝維申小姐，你知道艾絲黛拉的父母親是誰嗎？」

「我不知道，皮普，是傑格斯先生帶她來這裡的。」

當我從薩蒂斯莊園離開後，直接回到倫敦。當我到家時，赫伯特也在。

「河上的一切都好嗎？」我急切地問。

「是的，都很好。」赫伯特高興地回答：「昨晚，我和馬格維奇並肩坐了兩個小時。他跟我說了很多他的過去。他之前和我們聊天時，提過他的妻子，你還記得嗎？」

「是，我記得。」我說。

「她好像是因為企圖謀殺一位女士，而遭逮捕！傑格斯先生就是她的律師，那是他早期的一個案子，而且他也打贏了官司。這讓他在倫敦一舉成名。」

「還有呢？」

「馬格維奇和她在一起大約五年，他們生了一個孩子。他可能是對他太太不好，也可能不是這樣。總之，命案發生的那一晚，那個孩子，是個女孩，就不見了。馬格維奇很確定她死了，她母親為了要報復丈夫，就殺了女兒。」

P. 98

馬格維奇

- 你認為馬格維奇的妻子是誰？
- 你認為他的孩子死了嗎？
- 如果沒有的話，那她發生什麼事？

「這是什麼時候的事？」

「在他遇見你前大約三、四年的事。他說，你讓他想起他的小女兒。」

「赫伯特！」我說。現在我的聲音因為激動而顫抖。「被我們藏在克萊拉家的那個男人，就是艾絲黛拉的父親！」

隔天一大早，我就去找傑格斯先生。當我拿給他郝維申小姐所給的那張紙時，他很驚訝。

「威米克！」他說：「開一張九百英鎊的支票，拿來給我簽名。」

在我起身要前往克拉瑞克那之前，我將自己所知道和艾絲黛拉父母親有關的一切，都告訴了傑格斯先生。他當然知道莫莉是她母親，但是他完全不知道馬格維奇就是她的父親。

幾個星期後，我決定該是馬格維奇和我離開的時候了。我計畫沿著河，將船開到格雷夫森德，再轉搭固定從倫敦開往漢堡的汽船。我打算下星期三就出發。

P. 99

到了當天，天氣晴朗，但是河上吹著一絲冷風。赫伯特和我上了船，往格林威治划去。我對自己終究還是做了點事感到開心，而且在春日的陽光下徜徉在河上，是很舒服愉快的。

「他在嗎？」當我們快到克萊拉家時，赫伯特問著。

「在，」我回答，「慢一點，赫伯特！拉槳！」

船輕輕碰了一下岸邊，馬格維奇跳上了船。他帶著一件厚重的外套，和一只黑色袋子。

「親愛的孩子！」他把手搭在我肩上坐

下時，說道：「做得好！謝謝你們！」

當我們順著河划動時，絲毫沒有引起任何人的注意。剛開始，我們和許多船隻擦身而過。但隨著逐漸遠離城市，河上變得更安靜，鄉間景色也變得一片平坦。唯一的聲響，就是海鳥的叫聲。

我們停下來休息過一次，吃了點東西，但是很快的就又回到河上。太陽一下山，天氣變得愈來愈冷。我們得找個地方過夜。最後，我們看到河岸邊的一縷燈光，於是我們靠了岸，將船綁好。

P. 100

光線從旅館的窗戶透出來。我們走進去，向旅館老闆要了過夜的房間。那是個又小又髒的地方，但是廚房裡有溫暖的爐火，還有培根和蛋可以吃。用過晚餐後，我衣服沒脫就躺下，熟睡了幾個小時。當我起床時，風吹得很猛烈。

我們早早就出發，大約一點半時，就看到遠處漢堡的汽船。汽船正全速地朝我們開來。馬格維奇和我拿起行囊，準備上船。正當我們和赫伯特道別時，我注意到河岸附近有另一艘船，也是朝著我們過來。兩位男士坐在船首，另外有四個人划著槳。坐著的其中一個人，控制著船舵。當他看著我們時，另一個全身裹著大衣的男子，正和跟他私語著。

我可以聽到汽船愈來愈接近的聲音。這時，另一艘船就快要碰到我們的船。突然間，掌舵的人開口跟我們說話。

另一艘船

- 船上的人會是誰？
- 他們打算要做什麼？

P.102

「你船上有位潛逃回國的犯人，他叫阿貝爾 · 馬格維奇。我要逮捕他！」他說。

當他說著這些話時，他控制住我們的船，還把手搭在馬格維奇的肩膀上。這造成了汽船上一陣騷動。我聽見人們對我們喊叫，然後又聽見汽船停下來。

P.103

就在這時候，馬格維奇跳起來，扯下站在船首的另一個人身上的大衣。我只看到他的臉一下下，是那個較年輕的囚犯！康佩森！

接下來，汽船上傳來一陣大喊和水濺起來的聲響。我們的船翻了，我掉進了水裡。這一切發生得太快。幸運地，我很快就被救起，和赫伯特上了另一艘船。我四處尋找馬格維奇，但是都沒在水裡看到他或康佩森的身影。

當汽船開走時，四個划槳的人拉著槳，好讓船不至於翻覆。隨後，當他們往河岸邊划去，我們看到水裡有個黑色的身影，那是馬格維奇！我們抓住他，迅速把他拉到船上。他的頭上有個很深的傷口，胸前也有一道。我們花了好長的時間尋找康佩森，但毫無斬獲。

12. 新的開始

P.104

馬格維奇被帶往倫敦一家醫院治療。我獲准可以和他同行，在途中照顧他。我握著他的手，看著他。我所見到的，不再是一位危險的犯人，而是一個重感情、慷慨的人——一個比我更好的人。

他的審判安排在下個月。他病得太重，無法在監獄服刑，所以他留在醫院裡。雖然我每天都去看他，卻不見他的病情有絲毫改善。

在我人生這個黑暗期的一個晚上，赫伯特回到家告訴我，克拉瑞克要派他去埃及工作。

他說：「這是個好機會，我一定要去。」停頓一下後，他又說：「你有想過你的未來嗎，皮普？」

「沒想過，不敢去想。」我回答。

「我們在開羅的辦公室需要一位辦事員。要不要跟我一起去？」他說。

P.106

「謝謝你，赫伯特，這是個很好的提議。」我說：「但是，此刻的我恐怕憂心到無法做出任何決定來。我會好好的考慮，再告訴你。」

馬格維奇在審判中被判死刑。幾天後，當我再去探望他，我見到的已是垂死邊緣的他。我輕柔地拉起他的手。

「我的孩子！」他費盡力氣開口：「你從來沒有拋下過我。」

我緊握著他的手，想起自己曾想要丟下他的那一次。

「你今天很不舒服嗎？」我問他。

「我還忍得住，親愛的孩子。」

「親愛的馬格維奇，我要告訴你一件事。你能知道我在說什麼嗎？」我說。

他在我的手上按了按。

「你有過一個孩子，你很愛她，但失去了她。現在，她已經長成一位淑女了，她很漂亮。我愛她！」

他將我的手舉到他的唇邊，然後，他的頭就平靜的垂在胸前了。

馬格維奇過世後，我病了好幾個星期。那時候，我只記得喬的臉。喬在那段時間一直守在這裡，照顧著我。我身體好了些的那一天，醒來後，我發現桌上有張紙條，上面寫著：

165

P. 107

> 我回家去了，皮普，你已經
> 康復，不再需要老喬了。

桌上還有一張我全部債務的還款收據。

那天，我做了兩個決定，一個是到鐵鋪去感謝喬，另一個就是去向畢蒂求婚。

皮普的未來

• 你怎麼看？勾選是或否。
1. 畢蒂會同意嫁給皮普。　是 □ 否□
2. 皮普會回到鐵鋪去工作。是 □ 否□
3. 皮普永不再見艾絲黛拉。是 □ 否□

P. 108

畢蒂現在在村裡的學校教書，所以我先去那裡。當我抵達時，已經放學了。鐵鋪也在那附近。我看到喬和畢蒂在廚房裡，他們兩個人見到我都很驚訝。

「喬！畢蒂！你們今天看起來真體面！」我說。

畢蒂看著喬，笑了笑。

「皮普，今天是我們的大喜之日，」她說：「喬和我結婚了。」

我得坐下來，因為我突然一陣暈眩。當我感覺好些時，我才有辦法開口：「親愛的畢蒂，你擁有了全世界最好的丈夫；而親愛的喬，你娶了天底下最好的妻子。你們將讓彼此過上幸福的日子。我還要感謝你們兩位為我所做的一切。我知道自己一直惡劣地回報你們對我的好。」

喬開口想說點什麼，卻被我阻止了。我繼續說道：「我很快就要出國去工作了。我打算把欠你的錢都寄回來，喬。此刻，雖然我知道你做這些事都是出於你善良的心，但是，還是請告訴我：你已經原諒我了！」

「親愛的老皮普，」喬兩眼滿是淚水，說道：「沒有什麼需要原諒的！」

我們一起共進晚餐，隨後，喬和畢蒂陪我一起到驛馬站為我送別。

P. 111

當我回到倫敦，我賣掉自己所有的一切，到埃及去找赫伯特。我在那裡待了十一年。當我終於回到英國時，喬和畢蒂是我第一個去見的人。

這個晚上，我回到薩蒂斯莊園去看看。天色開始昏暗，皎潔的月亮已經出現天際。房子現在的狀況很不好，所以我只在花園附近走走。從喬那裡，我得知郝維申小姐已經過世，我還知道朱穆爾也過世了。

當我回想這一切時，我看到花園小徑的盡頭，站著一位女士。

「艾絲黛拉！」

「皮普！好訝異你竟然認得出我來！」

她看起來老了些，但依然美麗。

我們一邊走，一邊聊了好一會，然後她開口：「皮普，告訴我，我們還是朋友。」

「我們是朋友。」我回答。

我握住她的手，當月兒逐漸升高時，我們一起離開了花園。

ANSWER KEY

Before Reading

Pages 8-9

1 1. F 2. A 3. E 4. B 5. C 6. D
2 a) 1 b) 1 c) 2 d) 2 e) 1 f) 1

Pages 10-11

4 A
5
a) Not very good.
b) Small, dirty and very crowded.
c) Bad.
d) Dust.

Page 18

* An escaped convict.
* Hiding from the police.
* To cut the iron ring off his leg.
* No, he isn't.

Page 26

a) 5. The USA
b) 1. France
c) 2. French Guiana
d) 4. Tasmania
e) 3. South Africa

Page 36

* Estella is Miss Havisham's adopted daughter.
* She thinks she's better than he is.
* She wants Pip to fall in love with Estella.

Page 51

* He didn't want to marry her.
* She didn't leave her house after she received the letter.
* She hated them.

Page 66

* Yes. They were brought up by people who weren't their parents. Miss Havisham uses them both to get her revenge on men.
* Estella is proud. Pip isn't. Estella isn't kind. Pip is. Estella is from a higher social class than Pip.
* He must show her what love is.

Page 75

* He moved to London. He didn't have to work. He spent a lot of money.
* He became more ashamed of his family and was less kind to Joe.

Page 80

* Sad.
* He wanted Pip to be happy and successful.

After Reading

Page 98

* Molly.
* No, she isn't.
* Miss Havisham adopted her.

Page 100

* The police.
* Arrest Magwitch.

Page 107

1. No.
2. No.
3. No.

Page 113

3 a) 2 b) 1 c) 1 d) 2 e) 1

Pages 114-115

4 a) F b) T c) F d) T

5
a) Joe. Repairing a pair of handcuffs.
b) Mrs Joe (and) Uncle Pumblechook. Because Miss Havisham invited Pip to play at Satis House.
c) Bentley Drummle. He married Estella.
d) Biddy. She married Joe.
e) Compeyson. He wanted the police to arrest Magwitch and hang him.

Page 115

6
a) Pip stole a pork pie and gave it to the escaped convict.
b) Pip played cards with Estella at Satis House.
c) Miss Havisham gave Pip 25 guineas when he became Joe's apprentice.
d) Pip received a letter with a black edge from Biddy. In it she told him that Mrs Joe was dead.
e) Pip bought a boat to help Magwitch escape.

7 sensitive: Pip cried when Estella was unkind to him.

8 a) F b) T c) F d) F
e) T f) T g) T h) T

9
a) Pip was ashamed of Joe and he didn't want to see him.
b) Good.
c) Because he knew that Magwitch was a criminal.
d) Because he understood that Magwitch was an affectionate, generous man and a better person than he was.

10
a) Joe
b) Mrs Joe
c) Mr Jaggers
d) Herbert

11
a) Insensitive because she doesn't care about hurting Pip. Rude because she calls him a village boy with rough hands
b) She is beautiful.
c) Because Miss Havisham wants her to marry him.
d) She doesn't feel so proud any more.

12
a) Mrs Joe always invited Uncle Pumblechook to eat with them on Christmas Day.
b) Miss Havisham adopted Estella.
c) Joe married Biddy.
d) Magwitch and Molly were married. They were Estella's parents.
e) Clara was Herbert's fiancée.
f) Wemmick was Mr Jagger's clerk.

13 Miss Havisham gives £900 to Mr Clarriker for Herbert when Pip can't pay any more. Miss Havisham uses Pip and Estella to get her revenge on men.

15 a) 3 b) 1 c) 8 d) 2 e) 4 f) 9 g) 12
h) 7 i) 10 j) 5 k) 11 l) 6

18 For using him to get her revenge on men.

19 1. d 2. c 3. a 4. e 5. b

20
a) Pip stole some bread, some cheese, a pork pie and a file to give to the escaped convict.
b) Miss Havisham's father left her a lot of money when he died.
c) Estella made Pip feel stupid and clumsy when they played cards.
d) Herbert wanted to work in business.
e) Magwitch wanted to kill Compeyson.

21 *(Possible answers)*
a) lived with Miss Havisham.
b) she was unkind to him.
c) he was his best friend.
d) he arranged everything secretly.

Page 121

22 a) 3 b) 5 c) 4 d) 1 e) 2
24
a) blakesmith → blacksmith
b) neightbors → neighbors
c) trimfant → triumphant
d) apretnice → apprentice

Page 122

25 a) for b) as c) laid d) too
26
a) brought (Pip) up
b) giving away
c) turned out
d) go back
e) set off
f) turned over

Page 123

27
a) Who gave Mrs Joe a beautiful pork pie for Christmas?
b) What was covered in cobwebs at Satis House?
c) Where did Pip stay when he first arrived in London?
d) How much did Mr Jaggers give Pip on his 21st birthday?
e) Why did Herbert take Magwitch to his fiancée's house?

28
a) Uncle Pumblechook.
b) Miss Havisham's wedding cake.
c) Barnard's Inn.
d) £500.
e) Because Compeyson was watching Pip's house and Magwitch wasn't safe there.

Test

Page 124

1 a) 2 b) 1 c) 1 d) 2

Page 125

2 a) 3 b) 2 c) 2 d) 1 e) 4

國家圖書館出版品預行編目資料

孤星血淚 / Charles Dickens 著；Jennifer
Gascoigne 改寫；
林育珊 譯. 一初版. 一[臺北市]：寂天文化,
2016.9 面；公分. 中英對照

ISBN 978-986-318-492-8 (平裝附光碟片)
　　　1. 英語　2. 讀本

805.18　　　　　　　　　　105014830

原著 _ Charles Dickens
改寫 _ Jennifer Gascoigne
譯者 _ 林育珊
校對 _ 陳慧莉
製程管理 _ 洪巧玲
出版者 _ 寂天文化事業股份有限公司
電話 _ +886-2-2365-9739
傳真 _ +886-2-2365-9835
網址 _ www.icosmos.com.tw
讀者服務 _ onlineservice@icosmos.com.tw
出版日期 _ 2016年9月 初版一刷（250101）
郵撥帳號 _ 1998620-0 寂天文化事業股份有限公司